WAR BABIES

A NOVEL BY

Frederick Busch

A NEW DIRECTIONS BOOK

War Babies was originally serialized, in a somewhat different form, in *The
Gettysburg Review*, Volume I, 1 (Winter) and 2 (Spring), in 1988.

Manufactured in the United States of America
New Directions Books are printed on acid-free paper.
First published clothbound in 1989
First published as New Directions Paperbook 917 in 2001
Published simultaneously in Canada by Penguin Books Canada Limited

Library of Congress Cataloging-in-Publication Data

Busch, Frederick, 1941-
    War babies / Frederick Busch.
        p. cm.
        ISBN 0-8112-1103-7 (alk. paper)
        ISBN 0-8112-1476-1 (pbk.)
        1. Korean War, 1950-1953—Fiction. I. Title
PS3552.U814W37 1989
813'.54—dc20   89-35209
                                          CIP

SECOND PRINTING

New Directions Books are published for James Laughlin
by New Directions Publishing Corporation
80 Eighth Avenue, New York 10011

■ ■

To our friends and neighbors in East Winterslow

To Roy and Lil Cooksey in Torver

To Charles and Brenda Tomlinson at Ozleworth

WAR BABIES

*S*oldiers from England sang a song in the estaminets of northern France in 1916, and they had sung it too in the public houses, I have no doubt, of the Wiltshire I came to invade. They sang then that "Old soldiers never die; they simply fade away." That is of course what Douglas Mac-Arthur said before a joint session of Congress, shortly after Harry Truman relieved him of his command. He was fired in April of 1951, the same month Hilary Pennels' father was captured when the Chinese came across the Imjin River in Korea. MacArthur went home a hero, and had to decide between retiring a sacked commander or accepting the nomination for President. My father, in Korean prison with Hilary's, came home to face an American jail term. My mother divorced him after three years. I remember that I later recalled some smooth-voiced man on the radio singing, "Hey, there, you with the stars in your eyes" while my mother told me what she could about this person in prison in Kansas. I kept seeing a stranger, no expression on his face, and metal five-pointed stars over his eyes. I think I remember such a vision. I later saw a photo of the U.S. Government's Bronze Star medal in *Time* magazine—I was in law school by then—and sat up with a jolt to realize that whoever "you" was, with the stars in his eyes, *those* were the stars I had envisioned.

The journey to the cathedral city of Salisbury, Wiltshire,

in the soft, flat south of England, began with me and my mother in a bright blue kitchen sitting near a wide white plastic radio about as big as an oven. Hey, there, you with the stars in your eyes. The actual commencement of motion had to start in an Illinois town outside of Cairo, near the Mississippi, famous for nothing, or for its mayor, whose collection of Chevrolet Corvairs was said to be the largest in the Middle West. I flew into Chicago and rented an air-conditioned Dodge and drove to where my mother and her husband lived, near a proud accumulation of the most dangerous cars in America. I called him Bert, he called me Pete, I called Mom Mom, and we sat in the slick-skinned swelter of a Midwestern night in September, our forearms sticking to the red-checked oilcloth atop the kitchen table—chromium legs and white formica top, all shine and rounded edges—at which my mother and I had sat while my father was in Federal prison on a number of charges that included giving aid and comfort to the enemy during a time of war.

My stepfather was a huge man. His belly lay folded over the narrow belt of his dark blue gabardine pants, and his navel showed through the puckered buttoned front of his seersucker short-sleeved shirt. He had just come home from the bar he ran, taking a short night in honor of me. My mother was also tall, though small compared to my stepfather or me, and she looked younger now, in her middle fifties, than she had when she and Bert Bass had moved her household goods from Putnam County, outside of New York City, to Belle Plaine, Illinois. Mom wore lipstick and face powder, she smelled of the same toilet water she had

always worn in hot weather, and her seersucker housecoat
seemed to match Bert's shirt.

We had a snack of hamburgers fried up with onions, and
bottles of icy Hamm's beer. Mom and Bert laughed while
they complained about running the bar, though Bert slapped
his hip above the wallet suggestively, letting me know that
he did all right. Their house was cooling off now because it
was after midnight, and the windows admitted something
like a breeze. Still, we sweated, and we drank our beer and
ate our greasy burgers and we laughed. It was a fine night,
and my mother, who rarely telephoned, preferring to send
postcards from the bar—BERTS IN BELLE PLAINE, they said
in fancy script—on which she scribbled about good health
and wishes for cheer in the life of her only son, kept smiling and banging Bert or me on the arm as she drank more
beer.

So I hated to tell her, when Bert, with his usual delicacy
that came, each time he displayed it, as such a surprise (like
graceful fingers on a fat hand), excused himself, banged me
on the shoulder blades a few times, and went to sleep in
their air-conditioned bedroom. Mom was wiping her mouth
with a paper napkin, and I was declining a fourth beer. She
stood at their enormous refrigerator, which dispensed ice
cubes through a gizmo at the door, and then she shrugged,
took another bottle for herself and said, "Pete, what the
hell. I haven't seen you for six months—more? What the
hell. I deserve one more." Her voice was hoarser from cigarettes, and from who knew what she threw down during
the day at Bert's, when she tended bar and made the coarse

and cheerful conversation I had come to know more after her remarriage, while I was in college, than when I'd been a kid. "What the hell, baby," she said. "It's good to see you. It's always good to see you. What a hell of a big man you turned out to be. Skinny at the shanks, but nice shoulders. And I'm so damned glad you didn't grow one a those mustaches all the sissies wear. Guy wears a business suit and a cowboy mustache and all he looks like is a sissy, you know? Tell me, huh?"

"Mom," I said.

She stood at the door and rubbed her loose throat. Her eyes, inside the increments of flesh, looked as young as the eyes I'd grown up looking into. "You got a problem, baby?"

"Mom. I've been reading about Korea."

She closed her eyes, then opened them—it was her equivalent of a shrug, that slow-motion blinking—and she said, right away, as if she'd rehearsed it, "Baby, I can't stop you. I never tried to, did I?"

"Nope. You were always—you always left me alone."

"So I'm gonna do the same thing now, right? I mean, you didn't expect me to holler and wail, huh? Is that my style? Hey, you know me, I know you. You never forget. You never forgot. Jesus, baby, you never even *knew* to forget and you never forgot! So: you read some more about your father. You read about him, you worried about him, I don't know, it's natural, I guess, for a kid to think about his father. Okay. What can I do to help you? Didn't I tell you everything I knew? Baby, I only *knew* the guy four years outa my life."

"There's more data. You know how slowly the government produces things, its military histories. And I ran into some stuff about England, English soldiers—there was an officer I read about who was also in Camp Twelve. Where the Peace Fighters were recruited."

"Baby, I don't wanna know."

"Sorry."

"But you came out here to tell me, 'Mom, I'm goin' to take my vacation in England in September.' Go ahead. Tell me."

"It's busy at the firm. The court calendars aren't co-operating."

"They'll fire you?"

"No. I'm good. I bring in business. I get decisions. No. But they don't love me for it."

"Yeah. I love you. You know? And *I* don't love you for it."

"I wanted to tell you. I would have told Bert too."

"You're a sweet boy, but you're crazy. I'll tell him. You gonna stay a while?"

I shook my head and smiled. She didn't smile back. She didn't look at me. Whatever she saw was private. I stood— the jealous baby boy—and interrupted her by kissing the top of her head and tip of her nose.

She said, "Poo. You smell like a club car. You smell like a locker room. Poo. Peter, go *wash*, for Chrissakes."

She cried and I put my arms around her and hugged. "Aw, Mom," I said.

I was also hugging her bottle of beer, and it dug into my armpit. She said, "Tell me about Aw Mom, will ya."

"Guilt," I said.

She stepped back, as if my face or voice had changed. "Guilt? We—Jesus, Petey, not *us*."

"I feel like I did something wrong. I can't help it. I get other people off. Why can't I spring me?"

"All you did was get born, Pete!"

"And all my father did was—"

She put her beer down heavily. Her lips went thin as she pressed her mouth hard. She shook her head.

I said, "I want to get whole."

"Did I leave you in pieces, kid? Did he? Listen." She took a long swallow of beer and swallowed a belch. Her eyes were wet with tears. "Pete. Baby. Guilt's for the Jews and the Germans. Never touch it."

I was swimming in it. And at thirty-five, unmarried, a reasonably successful attorney who specialized in the pleading of criminal law, a man who might be called pleasant if not pretty, bold if not heroic, needful if not distraught, I flew into Heathrow and into strangers' lives at the end of September in 1984. Nothing I did would make that month or year the best of times.

In London I rented a small Ford that shivered and bucked in third, but went on into fourth and fifth and traveled in a straight line. I had two canvas bags and a wrinkled blazer, and the sure sense, as I left London, that I didn't know what I would do if I found Miss Hilary Pennels, or whatever her married name might be. How do you do. My father committed treason in Korea at about the same time your father, terribly wounded, was saving the lives of his men and distinguishing himself in the eyes of history forever. I just wondered if my father might have done anything to, er, kill yours? Hurt him? Betray him? Hello. My name is Pete Santore and I think we might have Korean connections. Hello. Hello.

The land quickly flattened out on the A30 past Staines. I drove sedately and did so, I realized, because, now that I was close, I was frightened of arriving. My mission was pointless. It had always been simply to be in the same town as the child of the hero of a moment during which my father had distinguished himself by turning coat. I drove into Salisbury disappointed at how brief the drive had been—not much more than two hours at moderate speed. I think I'd wanted to have to fight my way through dense bush to arrive at some outpost on a physical frontier. That's where you should have to go to visit extremities, I think I thought. Instead, I drove past pretty pubs and Tudor cottages and little brown council houses, and I saw the giant needle of the cathedral spire over cobbled streets and macadam, and buildings that were hundreds of years old, most either plaster-and-beam or flint-and-stone. The flow of traffic in Salisbury took me around and around the market square—it was not a market day, and so the square was used as a car park—and when I finally figured how to sidle out of the traffic and stop, all I could see were little streets and shops and a Westminster bank. It wasn't the setting for cowardice or heroism, or a confrontation between the heirs of each. Where, I wondered, should a war story—more extreme yet, a *civilian* story—be set?

I found the Red Lion Hotel, drove under an ancient stone arch into a cobbled courtyard just as coaches drawn by horses three hundred years before had done. Because I was an American, a tourist, uncertain of how long I'd stay (and therefore potentially a spender) they put me in what they called "the historical old section." It was old. The bed was on a platform, and when I stepped up to it, I saw ancient scars and carvings on the bedstead. The bathroom was up two steps, and there was something royal, to me, in stepping up and then sinking down, sighing, in hot water and lavender soap. I lay back in water to my chin. I fell asleep, slid down into the water, and gagged myself awake. Which reminded me of a man named Marino, an entrepreneur of real estate, whom I had defended against his children's charges that he, another stepfather in my life, had murdered the children's mother by drowning her. They based their claim on the only bruise on her drowned body, a livid mark above her nose. He had strong fingers, they claimed, because he had for years been a bricklayer. I tried to bring in witnesses with strong fingers who performed hard physical chores and who weren't murderers. The judge laughed at me, and disallowed the witnesses. The District Attorney's office laughed too. So, in fact, did my client. The judge, in a cleared courtroom, at a conference at the bench, had said, "Santore, are you trying to give the finger to the law?"

It was late, and the captain in the dining room was reluctant to even hint to his waiters and staff that I was there to be fed a full meal. He cordially walked me down the hall to a narrow sitting room of leather furniture and Oriental carpets and a fireplace I found too hot, and while I sat with the diners who had taken coffee and brandy there, a tray bearing a bottle of Château Clarke and two sandwiches, ham in one, roast beef in the other, was brought to me with dignity and dispatch. The waiter spoiled the ceremony by spilling the wine as he poured it, but I waved him off, as Americans always wave off servants, and I wiped at the bottom of the short-stemmed wineglass with my linen napkin. A woman who sat with an older man—he was telling her about the cognac she drank—had watched the proceedings. She giggled. I shrugged. I don't know how red I became, but she flushed straight up *her* face, mouth to hairline. I raised my wineglass. She motioned barely, with her snifter. She had deep-socketed blue eyes, a noble long nose, a lot of crinkly hair, a wide mouth. Her companion, who kept dabbing at the outside corners of his eyes with a handkerchief, stared.

I thought I heard him say, "Ping ping" or "Ping-Pong"— or Pyongyang, which was the name of the city near which several North Korean prison encampments were sited. I decided to settle for Ping-Pong and concentrated on finding a waiter who might bring me more sandwiches and then a pot of coffee, but only after I had worked at the wine for a while. The couple near me left, he with his hand in the pocket of his green twill suitcoat, she—tall, slender, heavy of shoulder and breast, self-consciously careful above her almost flat-footed step—gave me a quick smile as she passed. I started to raise my glass again, but she was gone by the time I had lifted it. Hello.

In the soft pudding of my Red Lion mattress, in my very old bed in the very old historical wing, I dreamed bad dreams and woke myself by crying out, and in the morning could remember nothing except dreaming in fright. It was

Wednesday, a market day at the square, I had read, and after tea in bed—Santore, going native—I put on a sweater and khakis and went outside to scout the hero's hometown.

The market square had been emptied of cars and filled with vans. Each had an open back, or open sides, and anything I'd heard of was up for sale—horse brasses and books, watercolors, etchings, old gout stools, new French goblets, as well as hot sausages, potatoes, fried fish, and a hundred varieties of sweet. Traffic roared its circle about the square, and the smell of fish fresh from Bournemouth and flowers from St. Malo rose with the sound of the cars grinding gears. Above everything, the thick brown tower of the Salisbury Cathedral rose, tapering to a dark needle, pinning the stupendously wide bright sky to the earth—or holding it close, at least, to where we milled and roared, bought and sold.

I was always aware of the sky there. It lay so wide over the world in Wiltshire, and often—as from the country cottage I came to know, and surely from the monumental fields and hills I soon was visiting—I found myself stilled to staring, to searching as I stared, for some word to carry with me that would re-create in months or years (for instance: now) the truth of how broad the land was, how deep and broad above it the sky that seemed more like a sea. I stood at the bottom of that ocean, then, and then I ducked my head. My shoulders were still up, and only beginning to relax, because over the surge and clatter and market day cries I had heard a hollow crisp *Crump!* It had seemed like something aimed at me. I forced my shoulders down, but heard it again—*Crump!*—in spite of all the noise, and this time I saw a set of glassware move as if in response. The woman who sold fire irons and wineglasses and ivory-handled meat forks looked at me and nodded, smiled with red fat cheeks that looked chapped, with yellow-brown teeth I came to call English, and she said, merrily, nodding, "Porton."

"What?"

"Porton Downs," she said.

"I'm sorry. I don't know what that means."

"American? Well. Hereabouts we have someplace named Porton. It's where the armed forces, kind of, test all their guns and all. Porton Downs, we call it. The proving ground. You can find it on a map. They shoot off guns of a weekend, from time to time. It makes the earth shake. I'm told the spire itself on the cathedral will move. Did it frighten you?"

"Startle," I said. "It startled me. I thought we were going to war."

She laughed and laughed as if I had told a fine joke. I thanked her, praised her forks, thanked her again, and moved on.

I saw an oilcloth of red and white checks that seemed identical to what Bert and my mother had covered their dinner table with. A sign called it American cloth, and I loved the connection. At a stall that said ANTIQUARIAN BOKS, I browsed among old green Penguin thrillers about wily lascars. The stall next to it had books, with finer-looking bindings, by Thackeray and Trollope and Kingsley, people I didn't read. There were curious books I did find interesting, and I was looking at something that studied, among

other things, the amounts of protein found in night soil
(the book called it) in Bethnal Green as compared to the
wastes of Belgravia.

The proprietress said, "He was Charles Dickens's brother-
in-law."

It was the woman from the coffee room of the Red Lion.
She wore what I later learned was a Provençal print skirt
and a white shirt that looked too large. It was tied at the
waist, rolled up to the elbow, open to the navel, and lined
with a cotton tee shirt, almost the color of her skin, that
made me think of skin. Her feet were in espadrilles, her
hair was pinned high, but it kept falling, and her face, as
well as what I could see of her chest above the scooped
neck of the tee shirt, was freckled. She was in her thirties,
and she blushed like a younger girl. I was in them too, and
I too belied my age by blushing. So we were onto something, we knew we knew.

I said, "Peter Santore. Hello. I'll take the book."

"It's fifteen guineas, and you couldn't care less about the
pollution of The Smoke in 1856—no, I lie: 1857. You don't
look like a Victorian scholar. My name is Hilary Pennels. I
own the shop. Well. This isn't the shop, of course. The
shop's near the close on the—you wouldn't know. I'll show
you one day, shall I? I also own these books, naturally,
since they're from the shop as well. And I wouldn't dare
sell you fifteen guineas' worth of book you don't want.
Hello."

I did not say to her freckles and her smile and long legs
that I had traveled from Manhattan to the center of America and over the Atlantic to London to the market square

of Salisbury, to see her on a mission of ignorant need. The shelling at Porton proving ground had begun again. I said, "This is like meeting in wartime. If I said, Hilary: we've only got a few hours—you know, the way they do in the movies? What would—"

She laughed a loud guffaw. "They don't dare say that sort of rubbish anymore, Peter. They used to. I watch those old black-and-whites whenever they're on. Do you? I call them weepers. I watch them and I start in shaking me shoulders and blowing me nose before they say their first *word*. *Waterloo Bridge* is best. Do you know it? Ah, sweet suicide. . . ."

I had stuck my hands in my pockets, and could feel a strain at my shoulders. I realized that I was standing as if under rain because my body felt under fire. I forced my shoulders down, and they ached.

I looked about, then said, with a kind of social desperation I hadn't felt since my boyhood, "There's an O missing in your sign."

"Yes," she said. "Some wretched boy stole it off me when I trundled us over to Winchester. They'd a sort of antiquarian books fair this summer. A terrible botch. Everyone bought Winchester thyme bangers, and no one bought a book."

"Time bangers?"

"Sausage made with thyme? What do you Americans say, 'thighme'?"

"Oh," I said. "No. We say thyme too."

"Time to what, Peter?"

It was showy and silly and like a gathering of law stu-

dents, that banter, but it was also thrilling because duplici-
tous—if I wasn't flying under false colors, exactly, I still
hadn't shown my colors at all—and she was charming,
seemed as innocent as all Americans like to fancy rural
English people are (except for the horse-jumping set who
keep being killed in country houses in films); and I was
aware that she was aware that my body reacted to hers.
We stood in the *Crump!* that I pretended not to hear, and
then it stopped, and I felt as if the blood had returned to
the muscles at the back of my neck.

"Did you sleep wrong?" she said. She reached around
and rubbed twice at the muscle between my shoulder and
neck.

"What would you define as wrong, Hilary?"

She did not say *Alone* or I'd have probably been in trou-
ble: would have had to borrow or buy a bike so I could
ride the edges of the square with no hands, calling her name.
Instead, she smiled, a good, broad, handsome smile that included me as a source of itself and she patted my shoulder—like a sister, or a wife, but not like a new romance—
and she told me to wander a while and have a nap and meet
her later on at The Chough.

Which is where we sat that early evening, drinking whiskey and telling stories—hers about the shop, mine about the
law—and feeling, I would say, awfully good. Something
exciting could happen, I thought. I kept wishing that she
hadn't been the woman I'd wanted to meet. I kept knowing that she was, and that I would labor to use her as well
as I could, as soon as I knew for what.

She said, "I'll have to tell you about Fox, won't I? I hid,

yesterday, when he came up. I hadn't thought to. He drove his rotten old Mini up from the motorway, and I was looking down the hill to watch him climb up trailing dust. I often do that with the postman, wondering what he'll bring me. I love to get mail, don't you? Up came Fox in his little car, more and more slowly. It was like watching a fat man mount the stairs—near the top, he'd hardly be moving. Now, Fox always rings before he comes, unless it's something to do with our hero. I'll have to tell you about *that*. Will I?" She looked at me, and I found myself looking furtively back, with lots of ancillary glances at ashtrays and embossed ceiling tin. "When Fox just pops in," she said, "you know it's about valor and something like, I don't know, the hillside in Twelve, the *good* camp, where the Chinese—Fox calls them Chinks—forced them to bury their dead. They put them in shallow graves, in stony soil, according to Fox. Of course the rains came in torrents, and of course they washed off all the earth. The dogs nearby were starved, naturally. The Chinese found them useful because some of the prisoners were frightened by them. So the dogs just sloped right off to eat whatever bits of dead prisoner protruded from the ground, as you might expect. And when I saw his Mini, I went upstairs and I hid. Like a baby girl. I really didn't want to know anymore. One thinks of the dogs grinning when the rains began. One thinks of an elbow joint or thumb in the mouth of a dog in the rain. I simply didn't want to know. I don't want to celebrate it anymore.

"Poor Fox! He should at least be a Dutch uncle by now. Sometimes, I can't decide whether he wants to be my father or take down me drawers and flop me onto the bed and fill me full of lead. Spread 'em, varmint, I gotcha covered. It's a wicked idea. It's too much like screwing your own dear dad. I see I've captured your interest, Peter. Is it the screwing part in general, the me part in particular, or the incest motif that strikes you as—what do they say in the States? Worthy of follow-up? Up *where*, is what I'd like to know."

Hilary licked her lips as if they were dry. Then she sipped whiskey and licked them again. She saw me watch her. I was trying to understand how much she knew about me, had guessed about me, how much of her friendliness was therefore calculation, and what I ought to confess. I said, "What's a chough?"

"Crow," she said. "Red feet. Is that like the crows in the States?"

I said, "But I *would* like to know, Hilary. About Korea. Your father. I'd like to know."

"Oh, well of course. I can't pretend to even be surprised. You know, almost everything significant—well, I don't *know* what's significant, do I, really? That's for someone else to say. But everything, then, that strikes me as *note*-worthy, that's it, ends up having to do with our bloody hero and his bloody ancient war. So I suspected it when I saw you looking at my books. I thought it even as I was thinking: What a nice straight back he has, what a pleasant, funny face. Do you believe in fate? You know, something that predetermines what you—did you ever read Thomas Hardy, Peter?"

"I, maybe—yes, in college. I don't really remember. A mayor, something. A lot about fate. He sold his wife?"

"Indeed he did. He sold his wife. And not all that far from here. No matter what the people in Hardy's books do, they're supposed to do it, you see. It always turns out that they've fled their own character, but their true selves catch up with them, and they do what they think they want to do, and all along it's been what they couldn't *help* but do. That bloody war. That bloody hero and his war. I always end up being part of it still."

"You mean I'm your fate?" I said like an idiot boy.

She smiled at me, an aunt's fond smile for a nephew. "I've been interviewed by an editor of *The United States Army in the Korean War*. I was too young, he was too old, poor chemistry; we didn't get on. He couldn't forgive me for not knowing all that much. I spoke with a historian at the Ministry of Defence attached to the Imperial War Museum. He was older. He had but the one leg. And I carried on a shatteringly fruitless correspondence with a young and stilted professor at someplace in America with a name like cheese, or soap. Now and again, some needy man, a Fox kind of soul, writes me or rings up and we talk a bit. Our hero is well remembered. I'd have spoken to you eventually, I suppose. Now I will."

"It isn't just Korea, Hilary. I *didn't* know who you were."

Her face lit. "Really?" Then the lights went off again: "Well, of course. That's what I mean about fate."

"Yes, but I didn't know."

"I'll take that under advisement. Is that what you barrister people say?"

"But I really didn't know."

"You Americans are always so proud of your naïveté or ignorance," she said. "But I do not want to live in 1951 anymore. Fox lives there most of the time, I think. He wants me to as well. Peter, are you really a lawyer? Really thirty-five? Really who you've been with me so far?"

I said, "I'll tell you my story, you tell me yours. How's that?"

"Howzat," she said.

"And what was all that bang bang, full of lead stuff, Hilary?"

She licked the inside rim of her whiskey glass and, looking up from under her brows, said, "Stick around, Peter." She closed her eyes and put the glass down. "What rubbish. I really don't want to get drunk and do my vamp—or is it vampire?—performance. I don't want to spill the whatyoumaycallit about my father because of Bell's whiskey."

"Beans."

"Pardon?"

"Spill the beans."

"Yes," she said. "I don't want to sit here and banter like some roundheeled intellectual. Could we go home to my cottage and drink tea, Peter? Or you could fetch something stronger along for yourself. Would you mind?"

I stood. I said, "I really didn't know."

She said, "Is that to be your battle cry? Rally about the flag, lads, I really didn't know? Don't be one of those Americans, Peter. Howzat?"

I followed her out of Salisbury on the A30 in my bucking Ford. She drove something high and jeeplike that she called a Range Rover, with the affection you use when you

introduce your dog. A few miles from Salisbury we ran
into September fog. I thought at first that there was a fire,
because smoke drifted in fragments, long oily strands. Then
it solidified and hung a few feet over the road, looking like
dirty thick air in headlights—which some of the other driv-
ers, refusing to acknowledge darkness, fog, or mortality,
still had not switched on. These dauntless commandos of
the night were unfrightened by zero visibility, and they all
but drove up the tailpipe of the staggering little car I cursed
at as it shuddered in low gear. Bert drove an enormous old
Cadillac, aquamarine, complete with high tailfins and a
three-year-old Buick engine; as Hilary slowed and pumped
her brakes, I thought of Bert and my mother—she had
learned to slide over on the bench seat and sit beside Bert's
thigh, as though they were teenage kids on their way to a
drive-in movie—and I thought how little my mother would
derive from anything I'd learn, and how much she wanted
nothing more from her former life. In certain ways, in ob-
vious ways, I was more of her old self than her new. In
certain ways, I was reluctant to admit that, and thus become a kind of parentless boy—*man*, I reminded myself,
driving in an English fog in the autumn, in my thirty-fifth
year: a man.

I nuzzled in behind Hilary as she turned right, onto a
bumpy rural road. All I could see, aside from white rocks
sometimes, or the low limbs of trees, were her lights and
the fog they illuminated. It was like traveling inside of a
cloud. I stayed in second gear as we climbed a steep hill—
no doubt the one that Fox, whoever he was, had climbed
only to be avoided by a hiding Hilary whose mind was full

of pictures of dogs holding human arms in their rain-wet mouths. I looked to the left, then down farther behind me, and I slowed, lifted my foot, stalled. The Salisbury Plain was below me, bright, as if sun shone, and silver, because it was the moon that lighted the long flat sweeps. Vegetation glowed, rivers looked like aluminum strips, and then there were great stretches sealed away by fog, as if lying under a kind of thick cream lighted by the moon. She honked her horn and I started up, then followed her lights farther, now turning left onto a fogless patch, a narrow lane crowded by hedgerow down which she disappeared.

I drove on, grumbling at having to be led, ignoring the possibility of crashing into something large and fast that might be heading down the lane toward me from the darkness of the trees that screened the moonlight and hid the Plain. I drove past her cottage, had to reverse and drive through a narrow wooden gate after I saw her standing in the lighted dooryard made of large stone flags. The high-shouldered house was long and made of brick and flint that threw off mineral lights as I pulled up, sweeping the headlamps along the stones. Thatch of the roof hung over into the bright dooryard, looking pale and frayed and nibbled.

Hilary waited at the door for me. She looked less nervous than she had at The Chough. But she looked unhappy, still. She was standing with her back to me. She put a hand on the door latch and turned, as if she had thought about it all the way up in her car, to say, "Are you in love with death, then, Peter?"

I'm afraid I sputtered and could say only "Well" once

or twice. That made her laugh, though I think she meant the question seriously, and she tugged me inside.

She laughed again and said, "You looked so *shocked*. I can actually believe it, you not knowing who I was and all. You *are* one of those Americans."

"And you're—"

"Oh, one of those orphans."

"I just finished thinking that about myself, you know."

"That's what I meant about *fate*, Peter." She pushed her baggy sleeves above her elbow and dumped her purse into the floor beside the door. "I'm an orphan and a sort of war baby and a sort of roundheeled intellectual, I suppose. I'm a ghost-sighter. I've seen them in the house—nothing harmful, by the way, only the great-aunt who left the cottage to Mommy, who left it to me. That's all I am. Well, that's in the eyes of history, isn't it? If you died of the question, by fire or drowning, or just, really, shock, I suppose, then history names you a witch. And all *you* thought was that you were a sensitive girl who heard these *noises* in your head. Or does that just mean you're the victim of mass hysteria, these days? I really don't know. I don't keep up. But, anyway, the point is—someone else decides."

She told me that she was assuming that I, like most Americans, regarded England as a museum and the English as exhibits, and she took me on a tour of the house. The floors were wide planks, except for the tile floors of the kitchen and bathroom. The walls were of plaster, interrupted by old dark timbers. On the same side of the house (one old shepherd's cottage, Hilary explained, of the two that had been joined to make the house) were the kitchen we'd entered, a dining room, enormous fireplace, and bath. Through a door to the right of the fireplace we walked into the sitting room, with its own great fireplace, a very few narrow windows, the stairs that led up. A door in the opposite wall was closed. And all of it was shadows and parchment-colored light, the smell of dampness and the sharp, sour smell of ashes and old apples.

I said, "I live in a three-room apartment. Flat."

"I know what an apartment is to Americans, you idiot. And"—here she dropped her voice, made each *r* hard, and parodied my voice—"I live in, to be frank, Peter, the eighteenth century." She waved her arm at the walls and timbers and laughed. In the same deep voice, she said. "You're welcome to my part of it."

I stood in the kitchen doorway as Hilary made tea. She didn't look at me, and I suddenly felt the occasion as social and she, for all her words and gestures, shy. I looked at her long pale arms, the long legs, the slight stoop of her shoulders. "What did you mean," I surprised myself by suddenly saying, "about being a war baby? When the demographers use that term, at least in the States, they're talking about babies conceived when the husband comes home from war. I used to talk about myself as a war baby too. I was one of those kids who grew up playing with guns all the time. I loved soldiers and weapons, war stories, I played with guns until I was about fourteen or maybe fifteen. My mother thought I was retarded. But what I meant, Hilary, you weren't conceived when your father came home."

"Because our hero died *without* coming home, eh? How

true. How true. Although, in fact, he did come home on furlough, I suppose you'd call it, before he joined up with the Royal Northumberland, the Fusiliers. They had room for him in the First Battalion of the Northumberland, or the West Yorkshires. He was desperate to go right away, Mommy said. He went into the Royal Northumberland and was home only briefly, bang bang he filled her full of lead, as John Wayne has said on countless occasions, and there I was. Manufactured in, by, and for the Korean War. War baby.

"But Peter, look at you, coming all the way over here on what? Your vacation? To ask an orphaned girl about a *war*. Come on, I'll pour a bit of this over a lot of that and put these biscuits on the tray—would you prefer a bottle of Worthington's E? It's a very good ale, although I keep it cool in the cupboard, not on ice. Well. Come on, Peter, let's tell one another some fibs. Or do you fancy a bit"— the voice deepening, the *r* in each word pounced upon and wrestled down—"of real hard truth."

In the sitting room, with shadows that hung from the timbers like fog or like dark cloth, Hilary sat on the low sofa that was covered with several plaid blankets of different patterns and colors. In the brownish light, they looked like shades of brown. I sat catty-corner to her, at the edge of the large stone fireplace. She talked about the difficulty of finding an experienced thatcher to repair her roof. I mentioned the Prime Minister, and she had the courtesy to smile. I told her a bit about the practice, and about my mother in Illinois. She laughed with pleasure at how I said what she had been certain one pronounced as Ill-in-oyse.

She had taken off her espadrilles and was wriggling her long toes against the blankets she sat on. She was careless with her legs, and I kept wanting to watch them.

But I said, "My father, unlike yours, came back from Korea. He was in Camp Twelve, which you know about, the Bean Camp. They named it after what they were fed—soybeans, I suppose. But they ate. They stayed alive. Unlike your father's camp."

"The Caves."

"My father was a traitor. You might know his name." She shrugged. "He worked with the Peace Fighters Battalion. Helping Americans and English decide to sign confessions. You know. Cooperate in any way the Chinese called 'Progressive.' He did that, and after the armistice and the prisoner return, he decided to stay there. I really don't know if he had a conversion, you know, really believed. *Thought* he believed. In some kind of Marxism. I always figured he was scared to come back. They made the prisoners who didn't want to come back stay in a camp that the Indian troops ran. They had to think about what they were doing, be talked at by their countrymen for ninety days, that sort of thing. So: he cooperates in a prison camp, but a camp run by neutrals—*that* one he breaks out of. Back he comes, good dog. They gave him twenty years. My mother divorced him after three. So there he is in Kansas, and some real patriot, a GI in for rape—he did a mother *and* a daughter in Tokyo. This guy breaks my father's back. You know, that famous moral outrage some people just have to express? So I'm an expert on Korea, and men like your father. Men like mine."

She moved her legs, and she saw me watch them. "In a way, you know, you remind me of the Americans I sell those overpriced and very available sets of Dickens to. You're so serious about your life. And of course in a way I remind me of all those women who derive great pleasure in telling American men how boyish they all are. Great fruity Oxbridge voices saying, 'Youth,' and all that rubbish. I am sorry. And I will tell you what you want to know. I'll get Fox to tell you. He was sergeant-major to our hero, and he lives more in 1951 in Korea than he does here or the present. Those Americans, after they buy those editions for guineas, not pounds, and far too many, some of them write home about me. Other Americans come and pay too much for carrying off too little."

I slouched and crossed my legs at the ankle. Hilary imitated me, and made a serious face that I guess was mine. I said, "I'll write home about you."

"I expect you will."

I drank more sweet tea with milk, and the silence between us rose up in the room until I looked at the ceiling, the deep casement window in the wall, then Hilary again. The house was murmuring. It said *Ooh*, and it sighed. I'm afraid I cocked my head like a cat or dog. *Ooh*, the house said. "Hilary, is this—does the whole house act haunted? Is that what we're hearing?"

She said, "Pigeons. The pigeons live in the thatch. The roof's alive, you could say. Would you have met up with me if we weren't children of fathers who elected not to quite return from their war?"

I said, "Sure."

"Liar."

"Truth, Hilary, I promise."

"Lawyer."

The roof stirred and cooed.

"I'm a sentimentalist. That makes me less of a good law-yer than I might be. But I can lie when I need to, it's an easy art to acquire. I'm not lying. I really didn't know who you were."

I slouched in the big soft chair and let my hand fall into my lap. It looked like surrender, and that's what I meant. She slouched as I just had, and let her hand fall as I'd let mine, and she made a face that, again, I assumed was mine. She laughed a kind of nervous bark I hadn't heard earlier, and her face went blank, and then was her own. She smiled a shy quick smile. "Good," she said, then left the room.

I have to confess that thoughts of peignoirs came to mind. I stood and went to the far wall, near the closed door, to look more closely at a smoky drawing in the room's poor light. It was of a middle-aged woman in long skirts on a very small donkey. A copperplate script said *Tuscany*.

Behind me, Hilary said, "That's by my great-aunt Martha. This was her house. She and her friend—her companion. You know. They read books and traveled." Hilary was fully clothed and was wearing an old dark green cardigan over her shirt. "Look," she said. She took my hand and pulled me toward the closed door. When she opened it, I saw a floor of old bricks, round at the edges, some crumbling. The walls of the short corridor were stuccoed. She opened a door to the left and a vinegar smell came up. Pulling a chain from the ceiling to light a naked bulb,

Hilary motioned with her hand for me to look. It was not much larger than a generous square closet, and it was very cool. The ceiling was low, and I could feel the light bulb's heat. On slatted wooden shelves made of old rough lumber there were potatoes, some sprouting, all with eyes as big as barnacles. There were apples and long hairy stalks full of Brussels sprouts. A few bottles of red wine lay among them. "Tesco's worst," Hilary said. "Plonk." Then she said, "Look." Beside the supermarket wine and potatoes were old wooden whiskey boxes, Dewars and Begg, they said, and in them were books. They stood in their boxes, which lay on their sides, as if on a library shelf. They were by Heinrich Mann and Wyndham Lewis, Willa Cather, Hopkins and Sassoon. I saw Edna St. Vincent Millay and T. S. Eliot, some pamphlets which, when I gingerly touched them, turned out to be issues of something I hadn't heard of called *BLAST!*.

Hilary said, "They're first editions. Autographed. My life assurance. Do you know what John Wayne would call them?"

"Are you going to say something about somebody filling you full of lead?"

"Oh, you are a romantic, Peter. No, silly. John Wayne would call this an ace in the hole. Haven't you heard of that before? If the shop threatens going bust, or if American mismanagement of the universe's economy throws us all into a depression, I shall offer these at auction in London or New York. The old girls would haunt me, I'm sure. They watch the house. But I would make out awfully well. Somebody will marry me, I expect, just to get his bibliographic great academic paws on these." She sighed. "But I am, actually, hesitant because of Martha and Mary Louise. They flit about, you know. Our Mary Louise, I can tell you, is no great pleasure. Her Harvey, her brand-new husband, was killed at Albert in 1916. It was rather a famous shelling. There was a great golden virgin atop the local basilica, and the Germans and English had their turn at occupying the town. When one side took it, the other shelled. And of course they must have aimed at the virgin. She leaned, and she leaned, but she never fell. Harvey was there. According to Mary Louise's diary, he was exploded—suddenly, she insisted on noting, into exactly six pieces. Have you ever heard of anyone's being exploded gradually? And how did she know it was *six* pieces? Well, she came to Martha for comfort, and she never left. A lot of the old girls did that. Can't blame them, really."

She turned around in the small cool room in which she preserved her fruits and vegetables and rare old books and she tugged on the light cord. In the darkness, she walked up to me and lay her long body against my chest and groin and even my thighs. She held herself there by putting her long arms around my neck. I widened my stance to hold us up. She was about my height, but as she stood there she continued to diminish, leaning against me and holding on, in that room where Mary Louise's sorrows were probably preserved on withering paper, and probably a record of Martha's late-found love. Hilary Pennels held on, in the smell of apples, and in my grasp, beneath the rustles and complaints of a thatched roof, and maybe the stare of the dead.

Beneath the thick afghan made of multicolored squares, each one knitted by Mary Louise or Martha—Mary Louise's were the finer knots, I learned, and they stayed tight, her ardor wove a constant cloth—we lay among our limbs and hair and breath, as if the two of us were half a dozen pups in a litter. Dawn shelling brought me up in a panic, pushing at the afghan, peering, saying, "What? What?" and for the briefest of times I was in a panic, not only because of the distant menace of that *Crump!* which shook the windows and burred in the wood of the floor, but I was panicked too, for that instant, because I didn't know in whose house and bed and odors and warmth I had wakened. Then I remembered Hilary. Then I remembered the proving ground. And then Hiliary had put her hands on my shoulders and had leaned her face in to kiss me on the breastbone. She whispered, "Have you ever had sex in a gunfight, Peter? This is your chance, old boy. Peter. Come on, Peter. Come on." All the windows rang in answer to the big guns firing. We shivered and hissed on each other while the birds in the roof cried out, whirred heavily into the air and came crying back down.

In the morning, later morning, when there was no practice shooting on the Plain and when a pale sunlight fell onto the bricks and high grass and apple trees of the fenced-in back garden, Hilary made breakfast and I hung around the kitchen to do three things—to watch her, to savor that she was there to watch, to revel in her wanting me to. I also did something else: I wished that I didn't want to take her story from her like a treasure I had crept toward.

She wore jeans and was barefoot. I went sockless in my loafers and wore the tails of yesterday's dirty shirt hanging outside my wrinkled trousers. Hilary wore something like a man's white undervest, but of a cotton thick enough almost not to be transparent. Despite her ranginess, her breasts were heavy, and when she looked up from the silly small square stove in the far corner of the kitchen, and when she saw me eyeing her chest, she reached up a long pale finger and touched herself above the left nipple, looking at me as she did. I rolled my eyes up and leaned back as if to faint. She laughed, and it wasn't plunder, then, but only fun.

We went out to the garden, Hilary slipping on a heavy checked shirt, and we sat in the sun that didn't warm us and drank coffee and ate bacon sandwiches. The garden was untended, and bright late-summer weeds still grew around the apple trees, although an ocher tone had cut the brightness of the grass. On a brick walk, on old wood-and-canvas chairs that rain and sun had faded, we ate our sandwiches, chewing loudly and happily, making suction sounds in our coffee cups.

"Excuse me," I said.

"Slurping allowed."

"Uhm."

"That was a glad noise," Hilary said.

"I'm a glad man."

She said, "And I never did split about our hero."

"Split?"

"Divulge. Give up the goods."

"Will you?"

"Would you stay here if I didn't?"

I said, "Yes," didn't I?

"Really," she said.

I said, "Yes" again, didn't I? Then: "Why do you call him our hero?"

She said, "You really did say yes." I nodded, didn't I? She said, "The vicar called him that first, unless Mommy had done so and I didn't know it. It's possible. She worshiped him in some horrible way. Along with the other feeling, of course. But it was the vicar, sermonizing, memorializing I suppose, in Salisbury Cathedral. The sexton's wife called him that in the fishmonger's off John Street—that isn't far from my shop. I already rang, by the way, while you were lying in your sexual stupor and I was commencing to boil up water. I lied a little bit about why I wouldn't be in. I did *not* say there was a Yank holding me prisoner in me bed. They stood among the salmon and sole and wept for our hero, as they called him. I did too, though I was very small. In town, in those days, it was unpatriotic not to. What did you call your father?"

"Dead."

"Peter."

"Not our hero, that's for sure. Not much, after a while. It was Daddy when we talked about him. When we buried him, the minister tried to call him by his rank—he had been a corporal. Italian Catholics like uniforms and ranks. My mother had hysterics."

"But you didn't."

My mouth full of bacon and pulpy bread, I shook my head, saluted, rubbed my stomach, and chewed on. I swallowed what I hadn't finished chewing and said, "I figure *I* was the hero, then. He had tried not to come back to me. Then he'd changed his mind but hadn't come back to me anyway. And he sentenced me to a long time alone with a busted-up woman."

"Well, Peter. It didn't all have to do with you."

"You believe that?"

"No," she said at once, shaking her head. She stuck a piece of bread folded around a rasher of bacon at me, took it back, ate one bite from it, then handed me the rest. "You know," she said, "I sometimes get to America on business. Well, that's nonsense. I sometimes could have the excuse to be there, I mean." I only looked at her and smiled, and she looked back. The telephone rang in the double peal that always makes me jump. Hilary also jumped. "That's Fox," she said.

"How do you know? What's wrong if it is?"

"Watch his face. He'll come here. He'll manage to come here. And he'll think his pornographic thoughts when he sees you looking like a rumpled bedsheet from our hero's daughter's bed. He doesn't approve of me seeing men. It's his idea I'm to be a kind of nun, one of the Order of Infinite Chastity on Account of Korea. He's responsible for me, you see. Thank God he's stopped ringing. He promised Daddy before he died, he says. I *know* he promised Mommy. He sat with her more than I did. I heard him promise.

Everybody dies, and Fox carries on for them. He's sort of a ghost for other people."

"Wait, I saw you in the Red Lion with him. That was Fox, right?" She nodded. "You were having fun. He and you looked fine. I don't understand. You're frightened of him?"

"Oh, Peter. You'll have to watch ever more closely." She put her coffee cup down so that it rattled on the saucer. She wiped her hands on her jeans and composed her face— pulled its features, somehow, closer together—and she made her voice harsh, deeper than in her mimicries of my American sounds. In these new tones she said, "The boxes, Hilary, were quite small, in fact. Handcuffed and shackled, the reactionaries, as the more resistant chaps were called, were stuffed by the guards, head between knees, *into* the box, you see." It was a different face and a different voice, and a different life that spoke through them. Someone else in Hilary told this story. "I have to say, it was appalling how long they would relish their work. A white man, if he had been conscripted for it, would have passed out, or wept like a girl. The bastards, as it happens, smiled." She coughed with the strain on her throat and then, in her own voice, after a swallow of coffee, she said, "It's like being beaten by him. He gets savage about it." And then, as if she slid by accident into the other's voice, her face shifted and the other voice said, "In that sun, they were half unconscious. Some of those lads, never mind the heat, dehydration, pure concussion, some of them, when they went *into* the box, had to carry their scrotum, if you'll pardon me, Hilary,

with both their hands. It was the edema, you see, from wet
beriberi." She drank more coffee, then cleared her throat.
Her eyes were full.

We sat a quiet moment, and I was aware again of the
pigeons in the thatched roof, the grunting of the large black
birds that stalked near the apple trees. Then Hilary said, in
her own voice, "I can understand requiring to know some
of it, if you think that your father somehow obliged you.
Parents often do that, don't they, and without meaning to.
You'll tell me about that, I think. But I want—" She started
again: "I don't want too much more of it, Peter, dear. I
really don't."

I stood and went to her and kissed her cold cheeks and
her hair and her long white throat. I kissed her mouth and
then went down on a knee before her and kissed her belly
and groin through the harsh fabric of her jeans. I said
nothing.

Hilary said, "I like the way you avoid having to answer,
Peter, you dog. You clever dog."

I panted like one.

She laughed and said, "Your lolling tongue. You dog."
And then she said, "I know you, don't you think I don't."

I slurped on my tongue and kept lolling. She pulled my
hair and tugged me up, and during my rise she kissed me as
if we were friends, dear friends.

And then she changed. I was to learn to nearly not be
surprised by the speed with which Hilary's face and bearing switched. I hadn't yet. I watched her eyes get darker,
her lids sink, the plane of her shoulders slide steeper, her
back curve rounder, her arms hang down at her sides. She

looked worn, but younger, and far more vulnerable. Fox was coming. She patted my cheek and went inside to make more coffee.

I sat in Hilary's garden on a fall morning in a country I'd not visited except for business trips to London, when I saw little except the insides of cabs, hotel rooms, and airplane lounges, with time out for pleasant restaurants that might have been in any big city in Europe or the States or Canada. A client's attorney had detailed one of his clerks to escort me to the Tower of London once, but all I could remember was a low room in a cellar where glass cases were filled with weapons. And there had been a suit of armor hanging from the ceiling, I recalled. A king had worn it. Our hero. Yes, the suit of armor, I recalled, had been on the postcard I had sent to my mother and Bert. A few days after I'd returned to my apartment in Manhattan, a card had come from Belle Plaine, offering a happy tit for my British tat: a cartoon-drawing of a Forties beauty in a swimsuit, who had just rescued a dopey swimmer from a make-believe sea; he asked her, "Will you save my life again tomorrow at the same time?" On the back, in my mother's crawling hand, it said, *Thanks for card. Love, Mom and Bert.* She had always been so healthy, I thought, considering her card, and healthy about so much else of her life. She had always been able *not* to fall in love with having her son to herself, and finally had run away from her life as the wife of a crime, and lived with a big-bellied man who let her tend bar so that her days were filled and she could never not be needed by someone, if only a drunk at the end of their bar who lived on shots and pickled eggs. I thought of her and Bert, and of their trip to the center of America without me. And, hearing the little voice sing its soprano *without me*, I wondered whether her health and her insistence on seizing it were what I might one day decide I had to pardon her for. It seemed to me, that late morning in September in another country, that when people learned to live without us, we had to learn in turn some way of forgiving them those flights, or of forgiving ourselves for hating those who fled. We spent a lot of time that way, I thought.

I heard what sounded like a self-propelled lawn mower, or a heavy-duty blender, and it took me a little while to realize that what Hilary had described as Sergeant-Major Fox's clapped-out Austin Mini had arrived. I stood and pulled at the tails of my soiled shirt as during courtroom argument I pulled at my tie. I heard his voice in the kitchen, and then I heard Hilary's, and she certainly didn't sound like the woman who hid from this man, and who knew his phone calls by their timing, and who avoided answering them.

The back door opened out, sooner than I'd expected it to, and Fox came. Hilary was behind him, carrying a tray. His hands were in his pockets. He said, "I understand you're a friend of Hilary's."

"Fox," Hilary said.

I said, "I understand that you are too."

He wore heavy orange-brown shoes with heels and soles that clicked on the brick walk—commando shoes, I had seen them labeled in London shops. His lightweight nubby tan tweed suit, his lavender shirt, his dark brown woolen tie, were elegant, and he wore them well. I felt in need of water and soap. He was taller than I, and very trim-looking, hard-looking. And I felt suddenly at home, if not at ease. For he was like a number of clients of mine who worked on the edges of television and stage production, and in the heart of real estate. He was not quite officially a crook. He wasn't legitimate, either. And he was an excellent actor therefore, and a pleasure to watch at work for a while. His face was lean and handsome, with a wide mouth and a long, beaky nose. His haircut was like a scar—short, cruel, stiff, and it made the healthy man look ill. The top was three quarters of an inch of dark brown; the shaved-looking sides, above the naked ears and long jaws, were white. His eyes were blue, and he stared when he spoke, as if making an effort not to blink. His eyes were very moist, and he wiped with a tan handkerchief at their corners. Then he smiled at me. On either side of five perfect teeth, upper and lower, was a mouthful of brown and gold rot.

He spoke in the deep rasping voice that Hilary had used, and once I watched her, as if I were a child who sought to catch the ventriloquist. Fox, seeing me see his mouth, said, "I never finished my dental repairs. Thought finally to keep a souvenir of the bastards. It was a stupid notion. They hurt like the devil, sensitive to heat and cold, pressure, *sun*light, I should think. I'll have 'em out and put a plate in next month some time. My man's on Baker Street, London—no more than fifteen quid a minute, eh? Malnutrition did it. I'd have lost a good many more of my choppers before this except—stop your ears, Hilary—there was a French cook at Twelve who fancied me. You know Twelve, of course, with your background. I was a pretty lad in those days. By then we'd signed up for the Peace Fighters Camp. This was after her dad had died, of course." I was going to see whether Hilary had actually put her fingers in her ears, but I couldn't take my eyes away from his awful teeth. His face came closer, toward my ear. I thought I smelled the smell of his mouth, like cheese gone very bad, but wasn't certain. He whispered, "The fellow used to, you know, suck me off. In return for food." Fox stood back and looked into my eyes and dabbed at his own.

Hilary said, "Coffee?"

Fox said, aloud, "It was a war. My job was to stay alive and help my lads stay alive. Of course, they separated me from them soon enough. In any event, it betrayed no one. Those Frogs had so much food, they grew fat as we grew thin. We *shrank*. They looked like a detachment of eunuchs after a time." Fox said, "So: yes, Mister Peter Santore. That is correct, to answer your question civilly. I'm a friend of Hilary's. I'm sort of her godfather, you might say. I look after her."

Hilary said, "Coffee." She stood before him, the heavy shirt unbuttoned, her breasts in the vest apparent, her shoulders slumped as if in submission. She handed him the cup and kissed him on his rotting mouth. It didn't seem a casual kiss. "Good morning, dear," she said to Fox, who looked past her face at me.

Fox wiped his eye. He said, "I know a bit about your journey, Peter. Hilary's told me something, and I can't hold a man's father against him, I want you to know. I assure you. Did see him in operation, though. Your father

was a slimy, treacherous, insufferable bastard, I'm sorry to
say."

I said, "Yes."

Hilary came to take my hand. She lifted it, kissed it, and
stood beside me, holding my hand in both of hers.

I said to Fox, "It's good of you to force yourself to say
it."

He said, "If you're after history, Peter, you've come to
where you should have."

Hilary squeezed my hand and said, "Peter has come
where he should."

Fox wiped his eye.

I can't say he didn't frighten me, especially the way he
slowly, constantly wept but with no expression. It was like
talking to a new creature, something from someplace else.
Yet so much of his bearing and manner were familiar. He
was like a number of men I had defended, or like the men
they employed: tough, interested in letting people know
how tough, and not reluctant to hurt you. He had to be in
his fifties, and yet he had the body of a younger soldier. I
wondered if he worked for a private security service, or
some paramilitary outfit, or the police. He had no judgment
in his eyes, no decision about me, but he made me feel
weighed. He looked at me as if I were a phenomenon about
which he would shortly arrive at a conclusion. And then,
I felt, he would never change his mind. His intimacy with
Hilary made me jealous—not only, or even, the way she
kissed him: it was her posture in front of him, the way she
stood, as if stripped. His hands were either at his handkerchief or in his suitcoat pockets, thumb out, four fingers in-

serted like a blade; they made me think of films, thrillers, of the heavy-shouldered man with long arms and hard fingers who hacked at the larynx or nose of the smaller man who fell and writhed and lay still. He wanted me to think of being hurt, as we stood in the faint weight of September sunlight above the Salisbury Plain. And I did.

Fox smiled, with all of his teeth.

Hilary left my side as his mouth widened, and she took our coffee cups and cream and sugar, though we'd poured none, tasted none, and she went into the house with the tray. Fox and I stood in the pallid light and the grinding of insects, the bass bark of the black birds, slight wind off the Plain, and we looked at one another. He dabbed his eye, nodded, then told me that I was a barrister from New York, how interesting it must be to see that criminals didn't go to prison—that was my specialty, was it not?

"Innocent men and women," I said. "Presumed innocent until proven guilty."

"Truly?"

I nodded.

"No," he said, "*really.*"

"Yes."

"Well, no wonder you like it, then. Good for you, laddie."

He turned and went to a small door in the brick-and-flint side of the house; it was toward the low end where the roof came down to within a few feet of the garden. As if he lived there, Fox propped the door open with a polished toe while he leaned and teetered, then tugged a heavy white metal table out. I went to help him carry it. He had waited for that, I saw, because he pulled the propping toe away from the door, swiveled on his other foot, lifted the table up in a kind of swoop and jerk, and carried it, upside-down, over his head to place it, with no sign of strain, and no sound, among the chairs at which we'd sat.

"I expect Hilary will have the luncheon by now," he said, smiling those teeth, not panting from effort. "I was going to take you to The Druid, which is a sort of a cross between an English pub and a bistro. The old man who runs it affects an earring and usually wears a leather vest with no jumper underneath. He smells a bit. Trained us for Korea. Called me the worst rifle shot he'd ever known. He did acknowledge that in hand-to-hand, the dirty stuff, I was as good as he was. *I* think I was better. I crippled his corporal just practicing on a filthy sand-colored mattress they'd flung out. He was grateful enough in the end, though he limps now, because I kept him out of Asia. The corporal, that is. The chap with the earring doesn't limp. He rides motorcycles with nasty boys and cooks for his customers at The Druid. You can sit outside and watch the Avon flow through it. Trickle, actually. It drips into Salisbury, and you can find it behind the car park at the Tesco market. Bit of local color." He wiped his eye. "But then I thought we all might stay here, since this was his house, where you've been—well, where you've *been*. So I chucked some wine and a few tins into a plastic sack, and Bob's your uncle."

And Hilary came out with another damned tray. It seemed that Fox's presence occasioned not only a change in Hilary's posture and demeanor, but an affection for even the apparatus of servility. I hadn't seen her without a tray for an hour, I thought. But there she came, and there was the tray, and on it were three open bottles of Côtes du Rhône—"It's the '82," Fox said, noticing my eyes, "very fresh still and unusually resonant"—and plates with pâté and cheese, blue linen napkins in ivory rings, heavy wine-glasses with pressed-in designs.

We sat. Hilary adjusted and readjusted her flatware. She passed a basket of brown bread. Her lips moved on one another, and she looked about with motions that struck me as abrupt—as if she expected to see more than apple trees rustled by breezes, and the dry-looking grass going tan. Fox sampled the wine, pursing his lips, swilling, sucking, smacking. He nodded, then poured the wine for us all. We sat, the wind blew, freshening now, and Fox, buttoning his tweed jacket, stood unblinking. He solemnly said, "Absent friends."

Hilary stood at once, head down, sullen-looking, but her glass aloft to match the glass that Fox had raised. Then I stood too. We drank joylessly to the dead, and then we sat. Hilary, as if she were obligated, chattered without pleasure about *chèvre* and the ripe little Camembert that Fox had brought. A *pâté campagne* with lots of garlic and chewy chunks of meat was sliced and smeared, along with the cheese, in nasty little trails atop the dense brown bread. Fox, who dressed so elegantly, ate with viciousness. He speared, he jabbed, he attacked his food. He hurried as if it might be taken away. He didn't look up except to locate the wine when he thought to pour more. He poured a great deal, and we drank what we were given.

I was looking at Hilary, who was pale, and who had

eaten little. I heard Fox draw a breath and heard his silver-ware clatter on his plate. Hilary, in response, inhaled as if she were wincing. Fox poured more wine for himself and then me. I took the bottle as he set it down, and I poured wine for Hilary. She looked up furtively, gave me a fast smile, then looked down at the wine she brought up to her lips. I heard Fox's breath again, saw Hilary wince again, and then there was the coarse, harsh voice beginning: "April, '51. Imjin River. Not Inchon, which you think you've heard something about. Imjin. It's nothing. Near not much except Seoul. Ultimately unimportant. Bloody Chinks and NKs poured over it like the Thames at flood. We were in support of the Yank Eighth Army. Actually, we were flanking the Gloucestershires, and we also had with us the crew of a British frigate who had come too close to shore whilst taking photos off the Yalu Delta. We had what was left of 'em. Gave 'em weapons, told 'em to fight or be captured. They fought, they were captured, and they were damned decent sorts throughout. We never knew what happened. We were bivouacked. They came in. We ran about in bloody circles as one is wont to do. Lieutenant Pennels knew best how to try and get a defense organized, I did what he told me, and they broke through anyway. Most of our crowd didn't loose off a shot. Most of them had been wounded to start with. Left behind when the others moved up.

"You know the Lieutenant did his best. We ended up, him and me, back to back. Defending ourselves with a bloody Webley and a *shovel*. They shot us to pieces. He took a wound in the head from a Mills bomb—hand grenade, whatever sort *they* used. Actually, that isn't impertinent. The Chinese, and of course they were in charge throughout, north of Seoul, had been equipped and oftentimes armed by Vinegar Joe Stilwell of the U.S. Infantry during the Second War. So I've always thought it was an American pineapple grenade gave the Lieutenant his shrapnel wound in the head. He took two rounds from a heavy MG in his arm. The bicep, stop your ears up Hilary, kept falling off the bone. The whole muscle. I'd never seen that before. I had one or two distributed about my person, and of course there were the odd nicks and rivulets, but they came from grazes and bits of shrapnel. You worried about them later, of course, because you could die of infection. But we were thinking first about killing them and breaking out. Second about not being killed in turn. Third about fleeing. Fourth about capture and surviving it. Then the pain. Ah. It was a very strong fifth, and rapidly gained first place in our affections, I can tell you.

"They didn't beat us when they captured us. Probably because there couldn't have been much of our bodies left unbloodied. They expected the Lieutenant to die, and they grew impatient after waiting half an hour. Then, after I'd tied a bandage from my kit round his head, just to keep the scalp from flapping so much, after they let me do that, they set upon me and did a surprising amount of bodily harm in a very few moments. I kicked one gook's balls halfway up his throat, I promise you that, begging your pardon, Hilary."

Hilary's breath, and the slow, frightened motions of her eyes—a kind of peering—were all the movement she made.

Fox, though, was galvanized. His face was flushed, his lips showed more of his dying teeth than before, and the stiffness about his neck and shoulders loosened, so that he seemed a happy man, even when dabbing at the corners of his eyes. He chopped his strong long hands in the air, pushed at utensils and plates, and waved his arms. I sat with my hands folded at the table's edge. When he chewed bread, his diseased gums bled, and sometimes his teeth were streaked with his own blood.

"The march was very difficult. We were conducted by what seemed to be a detachment of regulars from the Chinese Fourth Route Army. Bastards. They were so well kitted out from Stilwell's training—U.S. helmets, fatigues, packs, Garand rifles. It was, if you looked up suddenly, like being a prisoner of the Yanks. Then of course you saw their faces. They herded us in with Yank prisoners. You were fed what the Yanks called a baseball. It was boiled-up corn splinters and soya paste. They gave you one at dusk, and one at dawn, along with a very little water at dawn. Then you were told to sleep. That was all right. Except for the moaning and whimpering of the wounded who were in high fever. The Lieutenant never made a sound, I might tell you. He would not be carried. He walked, holding his bicep in place. You scooped up ditchwater if you were easy on yourself. Because you knew it would give you diarrhea. The splinters of corn coming out the other end—stop your ears, Hilary—were dreadful. You had to run ahead and squat. If a guard came by as you squatted, you were whipped with an M-1 Garand butt and left to die. Shit on the run, the Yanks called out. One of them loaded his trousers with his own discharge. The Chinese shot him out of pure disgust, I think.

"We were a week on the march, I reckon. I don't really know how long. I was suffering a bit, myself. The Chinese grew worried over how long we were taking. They decreed, after two days, that no one would be carried. You had to walk. If you stumbled, you were struck with guns, beaten. If you groaned, you were beaten. If your wound was open, you were beaten. In the hopes, I suppose, that you'd die and not encumber the march. We were told that we were benefiting from the Lenient Policy. An officer told us, 'It is lenient because we do not kill you.' The men held the lips of their wounds together so as to continue profiting from the Lenient Policy. The Yanks who were with us let their men fall. The British picked them up and carried them, in defiance of orders. The Chinese let them live."

Fox turned to me and said, "I always knew I didn't love the Yanks. You were careless with us during the Second War, and you were careless of your own. I always knew I hated you. On the way to Pyongyang I learned why. Do you know who one of the wounded was, who was dropped by his own and carried by us? Of course you do. *Now* you do, eh? The same one as lurked and skulked and hung about. Your father, Peter. I remember him well. We took turns letting him ride to camp on our backs. We did it as much to shove it in the faces of the Yanks. But we did it. And he paid for the ride, let me tell you. I'll be pleased to describe for you the fare he up and paid." And Fox suddenly stood, jerking the heavy chair back, pushing with his thighs at the white metal table, lifting his glass so that wine ran down its side and dripped very slowly from his raised hand. "Absent friends," he said. Hilary rose like a doll held up in reply. I sat still. Fox, above me, shouted down the distance between us: "He had a cracked skull, the Lieutenant. He worried at night, when we could whisper, that the germs were getting in to his brain. He said he didn't like it that his brain was exposed to the elements. Sometimes he forgot how to talk. He held his arm together with his fingers pinching the skin. The lice rode in his bandage. Your father rode atop the backs of my beautiful men. Rise, Mr. Santore. Stand. Get *up*."

I did. He held his glass at chest height. His hand shook. The wine spilled. His voice was low and breathy. Hilary looked at me and wept, and I drank.

When he didn't speak of the war and his captivity, Fox could barely force his sentences out. That was how I understood how drunk he was. His rage at my father, no doubt at me, and his possession—protection, I think he would have said—of Hilary, and the pure power of the facts he pronounced, all drove his language on. But when he sat, after forcing me to my feet—and I felt no less bested than when I was a boy and a bully kneeled on my shoulders and spat down into my face—then he became uncoordinated, weak. He knocked his wineglass over, and Hilary mopped up. He sat back in his chair for the first time that day, and he looked as though he might fall asleep.

But, like a man forcing himself awake, he leaned forward and said, "I wanna—I want you to hear more."

I said, "Yes."

"About the Leften—"

"More about the Lieutenant. Okay. Yes."

"Your father. Fucking father fucking father fucking father. Couldn't be drunk 'n talk like that funny farmer." He smiled. His teeth glowed. He sat back. "I have had a glass or two. Works me up, I apologize to say. Talking about the funny farker and my beautiful men who died."

"My father didn't kill them, did he? All of them?"

Fox looked at me. He said, "No, laddie. He left the great majority for typhus and beriberi and his other fine fucking farmer friends. A drunk wouldn't talk like that, would he? No. Your farking farmer friend of farmers didn't kill that many. No. Is that—was word, was—*what* is the word, Hilary? Ah!" He snapped his fingers while they held his glass, and he spilled more wine. "Consolation. Is that a bit of that, Peter? Poor boy." He raised his glass and drank.

Fox stood. He buttoned his jacket. He bowed to Hilary and said, "I shall be in touch, old dear. I've a good deal more to tell our friend before he leaves."

"I'm not leaving right away," I said.

Fox stared at me. He wiped his eye. He stared.

Hilary moved to kiss him on his awful mouth. "Drive very carefully, please, Fox," she said.

He bowed again and walked into the house. We sat at the wet, littered table, and then we heard the rackety bang of his little motor. As he changed gears, Hilary patted my hand. She smiled, and the pale girl disappeared. The tall, handsome woman with freckles was back, all broad shoulders and long neck, light eyes in dark sockets. She raised my glass and gave me a sip; I took it. She turned the glass so that she drank from where my lips had been.

We sat outside in a sort of silence. Everything else made noise—the black birds growled, the trees rattled in a wind that stuttered, then died—while Hilary ran her finger round and round the moistened rim of the glass we had drunk from. It screamed despite its thickness and heft, proving its value. I'd proved mine, I thought, by standing for the toast to the hero my father had helped to betray. I disproved mine, I thought, by sitting with the hero's daughter whom I probably would betray. What I wanted was her history. What she offered me was all the rest. I'd taken some of each. I wanted more.

She took my hand and pulled it across the table, so I leaned forward with it, until the table's edge struck my stomach. She pulled harder, then maneuvered her face and my hand until she had the palm up, and was moving down to kiss it. I retreated, but she held the hand, and I pulled harder, so the hand fell to the center of the table and lay, splayed, all fingers up and the soft palm accessible. It looked like a woman to me, lying spread. I took it away and placed it in my lap.

She said, "Poor Peter."

There are so many, I started to say. But I didn't know whether I meant *emotions* or *facts*. I went American on her instead, shook my head, smiled a rueful smile she possibly had seen in the films she liked so much—it was Gregory Peck under stress and shrugging it off: the psychic equivalent of a flesh wound. "It's only my mind," I said.

"You're such a swarthy, silly, attractive fool," Hilary said.

She stood. In the wind that smelled of apples and hay—it was a kind of sweet vinegar, innocent decomposition—Hilary unbuttoned the man's shirt she wore over the vest. She rolled her hips as she walked, and I followed her through the house and up the steep wooden stairs to the bedroom. Light on the small leaded panes was bright, unlike the sun that in the garden had felt frail. She sat cross-legged on Martha Louise's love knots, and looked young, very vulnerable, and compelling. As I knelt beside her on the bed, I looked at the door I'd closed behind us—old planks, iron hinges, a latch but no knob—and I saw what I took to be a sign. Closing it with us behind it, together, was acknowledgment—a contract, I declared, unaccompanied by trumpets and French horns only because I hadn't access to them at the moment. And, with a bare-chested woman before me, I stuck my legal hand out, but not to reach for what had drawn me to her bed. I said to her, "Shake, Hilary." And, solemnly, as if she knew what I meant, she put her hand in mine and squeezed.

We didn't speak again until I lay beneath the covers, watching her dress. Looking at me in a mirror, she said, "I like your long body. Are women all over New York City drawn to throw their lives away on you?"

I said, "Yup."

She said, "Gregory Peck?"

"Gary Cooper."

"Idiot. Cooper said 'Yes, ma'am.' "

"Yes, *ma'am*," I said.

"Idiot. Come for a ride with me. Oh, Peter! I never thought to ask if you had plans—you know, people to cross-examine, documents to search for, that sort of thing. Peter. I assumed I had you to myself. I feel so stupid. I would like you to myself. You had better not have plans. Shall I ask politely?"

"Hilary, you're my plans."

"Oh, I like that," she said. "Come with me for a ride. All right? Let me drive you to a scenic splendor and molest you on the way. I think I *am* a roundheeled intellectual. I don't know about the intellectual part, though. Why aren't you married?"

"Married?"

"Married."

"Well," I said.

"You aren't going to tell me you've a gorgeous wife at home in some place like they show on the television programs where the detectives live? All those dreadful gadgets in the kitchen and bikini suits on the terrace and she dutifully produces you a baby once a year? 'Hi, Pop,' they'd have to say when you came home from a *dread*ful day of saving crooks from their just desserts. 'Hi, Pop!' Oh, Peter."

"No," I said. "I never got married. I don't know."

"And you're not a pouf."

"A homosexual?"

"You couldn't be."

I said, "I'm not, I don't think. No. No, I never married anyone, that's all. Nobody ever asked me."

"Idiot. Come on for a drive, Peter. I'll show you something as lovely and dumb as you are."

So we went down to her dirty Range Rover, and we drove very slowly down the hill. She reached over and put her hand on my lap—she called it a more efficient gearshift—and my hips rose to answer her. Great tractors with closed cabs rolled over the fields. Gulls followed them as if they were ships, and the land was an ocean of light brown grain. I saw a yellow Labrador stalk a crow—or, more likely, a chough. And the sky had no bottom or sides, the land no edges either; the fields eddied out from Hilary's road in light and dark greens, the tans and yellows of crops, all cut by stone fences that looked, at this distance, like rock jetties at the shores of a sea. I had never seen so much of anything, I thought.

Hilary said, "You mustn't be too frightened of Fox. I mean, I always am, but I hope you'll learn to resist him a bit. He is *so* offputting! All those weighty words about wounds. All that muscle waiting to snap something. I always feel as if a tax assayer, or a customs inspector—that's it! I feel the way I do at a border of someplace. Here comes old Fox to inspect me. He'll know I'm carrying something I shouldn't. Except with Fox, he knows you're *thinking* something. And he seems to know me so well. Of course, he's known me just about since I was born. He and our hero were great friends from the start. Part of making your men a part of your life," she said in a gruff military voice. Then in her own: "Fox was at the cottage all the time after Korea, when he came back. He was a great help to Mommy. She loved him. He loved her. You know. Do you? What I mean, dear, is that they *loved* each other. You know. Anyway, we're away from him. He'll go pottering home in his horrible car and drink more wine in his terrible flat. He lives outside Winchester and drives here in third gear because he thinks so much about our hero and Mommy and me that he forgets to shift. He told me that. I twitch my nose at him when he says that sort of rubbish. Watch tomorrow when he comes. I'll twitch my nose and he'll stop. It's something about the nose itself, actually. You'll see.

"We're going to Britain's monument, Peter. I want to show you Stonehenge. It's got all sorts of fences and wires round it, but it's quite beautiful, still. You know, when I was a girl, we could run and play on the stones themselves. No one cared. Oh, there'd be the odd initial carved into the rock, that sort of vulgarity, but nothing importantly awful. Then, in the Seventies, a group of wild-eyed hippy squatters descended upon it. They said they were claiming it in the name of the people. I never trust anyone who does anything in the name of the people, do you? They camped there. Police vans all round, lights and Alsatians and TV cameras everywhere. When they left, at last, they had sprayed their names and stupid slogans on those great, lovely, timeless rocks. No one knows how they came there still, you know. Taken on boat from Wales, then rolled on logs overland, that's one theory. The stones do seem to be Welsh. Mommy always said it seemed like something perverse only the Welsh would do. Need I tell you that Fox is Welsh? So there it was. They had to sandblast the skin of all that history off the poor stones. That was when they put fences and wires round it all and round each stone.

"When I was a baby I used to wear red rubber boots and I used to dance on the sacrifice stone. That was before they got rational and talked about cosmic observatories and all of that. People believed the Druids sacrificed virgins to celebrate the death of the year, and to pray the sun would come back after winter. People all rigged out in white robes come, still. They dance about and hold knives up in the air, look like a bunch of crazy spinsters, or your Ku Klux Klan. But in *Tess of the D'Urbervilles*—you've read that? Oh, Peter, you *must!* It's my most favorite read of *all* time. Listen. Hardy believed in the Druids. Or in the belief in them, at any rate. And at the end, there's Tess, all pale, a kind of bride, you see, all stretched out on the sacrifice stone, the one they thought the virgins were killed on. Of course, she isn't a virgin anymore. That's part of it. She was betrayed in her *sleep*, Peter. Could we try that some time? I'd love it if you betrayed me in my sleep. Could we

do it asleep, dear? And Angel has come to love her truly.
They're in flight from the sheriff, I forgot to tell you that.
Anyway, she sleeps and he stands guard above her at Stonehenge. Comes the dawn, and the sheriff's men come riding
from every direction. And there's Tess, bride of death,
lying on the sacrifice stone. It's all but pornographic, it's so
marvelous. It's her fate, you see. Come see the stone."

It rose up beside the A303, at first so small as to be dis-
appointing. I sat in the car with my legs apart because
Hilary was playing gearshift with me. But I put my legs together when I saw the dark rocks in their crazy circle. We
parked, and Hilary, like a child at an amusement park, led
me through a tunnel that crossed beneath the roadway to a
ticket window. She paid for us, and we walked more slowly
between fences to the thigh-high black wire that encircled
each stone, and that went around each ring of stones as
well. I followed Hilary's quick march counterclockwise
and then stopped behind her. She was teetering on her
toes—they were in American running shoes—and looking
at a long, coffin-sized stone that was at right angles to us.
It looked like blue-black rock and nothing more. The
stones against the sky were spectacular—dark, immense,
purposeful, and secret. The stone we stood at was like a
bad imitation of a sarcophagus. Tourists in bright wrinkled
cloth walked, murmuring, and I heard German and French
while we stood there. An American man said, "Laynie!
Look! *Laynie!* Watch the sun come through it!" The low
sun lay on one of the high lintels balanced on two great
vertical stones. The American was repaid, for the sun at
Stonehenge had performed as warranted. "See?"

Hilary said, loudly, "Druids raped virgins here. They were big rutting fanatics, not some kind of scientist."

The American, a trim tanned man whose blond hair was sprayed into place—it matched his wife's, I thought—stared at Hilary with scorn.

She felt it, she had wanted to excite it, and she turned and said to him, "It was very priapean, and had little, I'm afraid, to do with the collection of data. I'm a native. I know this for fact." She turned her back on him, put her lips to my ear, kissed it, whispered, "The sacrifice stone, Peter," and I knew what she was going to do.

"No," I said. "Hilary, dammit, no."

She put her slender brown wallet into my hand, then slowly climbed over the wire. Someone said something in Japanese. She stood beside the rock and said, "I used to dance on this in red boots." She sat on the stone as if it were a bed. I saw the guard in his dark blue uniform come walking from the far diameter of the circle. He rose between the stones. She lay down and she folded her hands at her waist and closed her eyes. I saw the lids flicker.

The guard said what guards in England always seemed to say: "Oi!"

Hilary said, "Yes. The sheriff's men."

She sat up, pushed at her hair, said, "Good morning" to the guard, who stood beside me. I smelled his perspiration and his shaving lotion.

"Get out," he said. "This is a national monument, miss."

"Oh," she said. "Don't we change for the Northern Line here? You mean this *isn't* Chalk Farm?"

"All right," the guard said. His fat face was pale. I worried for his health. "I shall be forced to take your name, miss." He turned to me. "What's her name, sir. Do you know?"

"No," I said, visiting American smartass, "no, but she looks local."

He had a pad and pencil ready. He jerked his thumb at her. "Out."

Hilary said to me, "Remember this." She lay back down and closed her eyes. Then she sat up, slid from the stone, walked over the wire, said "Sorry" in passing the guard, as if she had coughed in a theater, and led me to the car. The guard followed us, and the American couple followed the guard. They told him that the strange woman had desecrated a great ancient observatory. Hilary, standing at her Rover as if for a photo to be taken by the guard, said, "*Druids*. Stone knives. Torn virgins. Can't you *remember?*"

The Americans turned away. Hilary waved to the guard, who closed his book and walked off. She said to me, "You remember, Peter. If you forget, he's taken notes, I think." We got into the Range Rover, and she drove us away. She laughed once, but when I didn't join her, she grew quiet and she looked at only the road.

After a while, Hilary said, "Your father didn't kill him, Peter. I think I know that."

"He was there at the killing, though. Wasn't he?"

"Sort of, I think. Not in an important way, though. I'm taking us back to the cottage so I can change. Then we'll go to the Red Lion so you can change. Want me to give yer

a barf, ducks, heh heh? And then you can treat us to drinks
and a very good dinner and brandy and—are you in the old
section or the new wing? Are you over the courtyard?"

"I think so, yes. The bed's old as hell."

"Oh, I love that. We'll have lots of brandy and go up
to bed in the seventeenth century. Will you invite me?"

"Hilary—"

"Do I drive you mad?"

"A little, yes. But I was going to say: I would give you
pretty much whatever you wanted, I think. Even if I didn't
want to. And I hadn't intended to want to."

"Darling, that's very good. You're falling under my spell.
It isn't just that I speak two languages well and one passably
and own a thriving small business plus a decent old cottage
in the country. It's my physique, isn't it? And my knowledge of ze ahrts of love? Peter, whatever I say tonight, do
not let me order the curry. It's good, mind you, but I never
taste the wine when I eat the curry at the Red Lion.
They've a chef from the Punjab or somewhere, and he
must have a tongue of iron. Oh, my, that would be painful.
Besides, I ate the curry two nights ago, you know, while
you were waiting to spring out at me. I want quail if they
have it. Pheasant. Even pigeon pie. No: duck. Something,
you know, gamey. I want something I can really taste, and
a marvelous green young hock that's very fresh, or something old and red from Burgundy that costs a great deal.
Which do you think?"

I was thinking about the soybean and corn kernels splin-
tering in the bowels of sick men who were gunwhipped as

they squatted and bled while the column shuffled past. I was thinking of Lieutenant Pennels, Hilary's father, holding his bicep onto his arm and worrying that the lice in the bandage at his head wound were invading the bruised soft coils of his brain. I saw Fox, wounded and bloody and beaten and somehow still competent, strong. I saw my father, a pouting boy with an army haircut in an overexposed newspaper halftone. I saw him riding in a fireman's carry on a wounded English soldier's back. I saw myself on Hilary, under the comforter tied for love by Mary Louise and Martha, Wiltshire ghosts. I thought of being ridden, too, while cannon fired and the house thumped.

Hilary said, "Peter, *don't*. Don't. You aren't—Peter, you've done nothing *wrong*."

I waited in Hilary's sitting room while she changed her clothes. Martha and Mary Louise did not come dripping from the ceiling or wailing from the cracks between the floor planks. No cannon went off, though a couple of low-flying jets rattled the windows. She wore a black cotton shirt and a black long skirt, black boots, black tights, a wide band of jet about her long exposed neck, and she carried a large brown leather bag that didn't match anything she wore. She swung it, like a girl coming home from classes. "Underwear," she said. "Sundries, intimates, a five-pound note in case you throw me out, anything you'd need for staying with a man at his hotel. I'm invited to stay, I assume. At this point you say"—it became Jack Palance's bullying voice, low and slick—"you damned well better."

"Yes," I said. "Kindly."

"*Kindly*," she said in Hilary's voice. "You're so *sweet*, Peter. I could eat you up." She took my arm as we walked to her car. She kissed my neck and said, "Yum."

We drove through back roads, where what I saw were mostly lanes, and hedgerows, little front gardens, one of them tended by a fat young man with his shirt off and a cigarette in his red face glowing. Then Hilary turned onto a motorway, and in the almost-darkness I saw what seemed to be a sign with a tractor's silhouette painted on it. We came to another, and I saw that the sign showed a tank.

Hilary said, "Tank crossing."

I thought of deer leaping across country roads at deer crossings. I had seen snowmobile crossings in the Adirondacks, and pedestrian crossings, of course, with silhouettes of tiptoeing walkers or children at play. I'd seen cattle crossings near Belle Plaine. So I thought of tanks, crossing daintily, their treads working as legs—Disney tanks—to get them from one side of the road to the other. At the Red Lion, while Hilary ate chicken cooked with lemon, and while I ate the curry to kill the taste of a Moselle bottled, I thought, at Penzance or Birmingham, I imagined tanks scuttling across the motorway. Why does a tank cross the road?

We went up to bed. I said, to the tall naked woman flinging her shoe at a far wall, as I admired the muscles in her long back and high buttocks—as I admired that she was *here*—"I never climbed up into the sack before."

Hilary lay on the bed. Her legs were crossed at the ankle. Her hands were at her waist. She looked like the virgin on the rock at Stonehenge, who once had danced there in red rubber boots. She looked easy, as if we were old friends now, familiar lovers, people we could trust. She said, "Sack means to pillage, you know, in a war? You never had to read anything in school, did you? Except law, I suppose. You didn't read John Donne, did you? Holy Sonnet Fourteen? It would appeal to your—male sense of things, I wager. Poetry can be very sexy, you know. Of course, this one's holy, it's religious, a kind of prayer, you see. But it's also a *nasty* bit of holy sex. He prays to God and says, 'Take me to you, imprison me, for I / Except you enthrall me, never shall be free, / Nor ever chaste, except you ravish me.' You see he's a city inviting the sack. And then he becomes a woman. She invites him to rape her. What— Peter? What d'you think of things like rape? Lying on a woman and forcing her legs apart? Peter. Come on, Peter. Come on."

We slept straight through, smelling of sex and curry and lemon and wine, and we were wakened on the soft bed, built at about the time John Donne, I figured, was writing a poem to God and Hilary on love's strong measures. A tense, sweating chambermaid knocked and came in, bringing dark tea and sour underdone scones that were hot enough to melt sweet butter. Hilary showed me the toothbrush that she'd brought, but she insisted on brushing her teeth with mine. She came back wearing my yesterday's dirty shirt, and we sat up in bed to drink more tea.

Santore, the tireless examiner: "Did you promise Fox you'd tell me things, Hilary? You know—"

Her face softened. Her lower lip dropped the slightest bit. Then she tightened and said, "No, sweet Peter, I did

not. I had, in fact, decided to say what I could to you.
About it. To save you having to hear it from him. He'll
catch up with us before you leave me at the quay, weeping
while your ship steams out. Whatever you're going to do
to me. Oh, don't you work your wiles at me, white man, I
know you sailors and your ways. Peter, no, it's just he's so
brutal about it. He loves to tell it all, as painfully as he can."

"Why not? He went through—he and your father went
through so much. How can you recover from that?"

"I should think it's one's duty to, as you say, recover.
From one's past. Mind you, I don't know how easy it
might be. But you should make the effort. You should
prosper in the wake of your past, not live a cripple. England's full of cripples. It's the country of cripples. You see
them all over the towns, in braces and wheelchairs and with
no arms, wheezing and spitting blood and falling over in
pubs. Why can't we be *healthy?*" She slid a warm and
smooth long thigh over mine. "I'm healthy."

"Aren't you. I didn't know so much health could happen."

"Your Vietnam veterans, wearing their hair long and
being so neurotic—"

"Hilary, they had a really bad time."

"Yes," she said. "Didn't we all. You'd say *no*. You're
feeling too guilty to say yes. Say yes, Peter."

"Yes."

"Shall I tell you before Fox does? Or should we batter
each other's heart and, as I recall it saying—the poem I told
you about? By Donne? There's something about break, and
burn, and blow. I could tell you that. Hmm?" She turned

in the bed, but only to look at me, I think. Because she said, "*Peter*," as a mother might, or a wife.

"I wasn't crying, I was laughing."

She said, "Tell me what you were laughing at. Have a crumb of scone and a thimbleful of tea and tell me what you were laughing at."

"I was remembering my father's letter, this letter he sent home. When he was in prison. He told my mother to raise me like a man of the world, not just America. So, I was thinking—here I am. A man of the world. That's all."

"But that isn't funny, sweetheart. Is it?"

"Well, Hilary. You don't always laugh at what's funny. Sometimes people just laugh. Sometimes they laugh at what's sad."

"Is it what you do instead of weeping?"

"Tell me about The Caves."

"Promise that you won't leave, directly I've told you those things. They're dreadful."

"I promise."

"You do swear and affirm—I saw that in a film one night on television, it was an American movie about racialism, as I recall."

"Swear and affirm, Hilary."

"Kiss me, please. A token of later goodwill."

We kissed and then turned sideways to each other, lying back against the pillows, looking into the gold September light that lay on darkened wood and dusty white walls. Hilary told me.

It began in Camp Nine, The Caves, when my father, Corporal Santore, came from the Bean Camp, number

Twelve, where Colonel Kim was organizing a Peace Fighter Camp. He sent Chinese interrogators, North Korean guards, and my father, who had long before volunteered his services. He'd already been telling the Chinese officers what his friends spoke of at night, and how they thought about escaping. (They didn't; they were dying slowly, and too weak and ill to sleep, much less flee on foot.) Colonel Kim's offer to the men at The Caves consisted of good food, medical attention, bedding, clothing, cigarettes, soap. The men lived in and on small creeks that ran through the dark, long, low cold caves. They were lice-ridden, and they suffered from beriberi, dysentery, and pellagra. Their wounds were infected. They moaned and wept and then went silent and curled themselves into a fetal position and died. Some men—mostly Americans—stole dead men's food. Some men—mostly British—cleaned the sick men, pulled them into the sunlight when they were allowed to, and even picked the lice from their head and chest and wounds. The men with beriberi swelled—legs, thighs, loins, stomach. They tried to sleep sitting up, to relieve the pain of the pressure of the fluids that filled them. But they were weak, and they fell over and drowned in the fluids produced by beriberi pneumonia. Others bled from the gums and urinary tract, whimpered from bone pain and cramps while they slept.

Officers had been separated from enlisted men, but the Lieutenant, a man soon to die, was left to lie with his head on Fox's sweater. Fox was to be taken to another camp when the Peace Fighters team left. The men, without leadership, so the Chinese figured, would cooperate more readily.

Lieutenant Pennels lay in the cold mud and bat droppings at the rear of the cave. He was alert, Fox had told Hilary's mother after the repatriation. His eyes were open, and he listened. At night, he whispered instructions to Fox, who passed them to the men. They obeyed, they held inspections of wounds, demanded a cleaning-up, within reason, of every man in the cave, conducted discussions of ways to resist since resistance was their obligation. A private, a cook's helper, was dragged from the cave for resisting by spitting into the face of a Chinese interrogator. A hoist of square timbers was erected in the sunlight outside their cave. The private's hands were tied behind his back. He was lifted, screaming, by a rope that went over the high hoist and was knotted to the rope behind his back. They heard his shoulders dislocate, his collarbones crack, his wrists break. The North Korean guard, behind the hoist, climbed the rope as the private shrieked, and he jumped up and down to yank the rope, as if he were ringing a bell. The bell screamed and screamed. I must be making it up, I wasn't there. Hilary only said: he was hanged by his hands which were tied behind his back. My father was there and certainly witnessed the torture, must have heard the private scream as they let the guy down. He was one of the men who lay still for a while and then died.

Sitting back, choking sometimes on what she said, I looked at her grand, long nose, so delicately made. Her lovely mouth said dreadful words. And then I was hearing her brilliant mimicry, this time of a Chinese interrogator she could only have heard about. He was saying, "Tell me your opinions of the Chinese People's Volunteers. What do you feel about your life in this camp? Are you happy here? How happy are you with our rations? Why are you fighting so far from your home, side by side with Mei-kuo? Do you understand how wrong you are to take part in Korean war? Speak freely. Do not fear us. You may express your opinion without fear."

The final offer was made. Join the Peace Fighters, make propaganda broadcasts, sign petitions for peace and the condemnation of Allied efforts, or lie in the caves and eat soya meal once or twice a day, drink water from a well a dozen yards from the Chinese officers' latrine, pick lice and get gangrene, choke on your body's liquids, die. The men were exhausted, their number down to eighteen British and six American enlisted men, a sergeant, and an officer whose arm and head were open to the air. Lieutenant Pennels whispered to Fox, and Fox told the Yanks and his men. The Lieutenant says that you can be half-hearted with the Chinks and survive. You can sign a few papers and claim coercion, torture. The Lieutenant says this *is* torture. The Lieutenant says that he loves you as brave fighting men and won't see you further degraded. He says to remember your duty is subtle but steadfast resistance once you've gone to Camp Twelve. He says try to escape. He says first get strong and healthy on the rations. Get medical help. Demand it. When they give you lectures on communism, the Lieutenant says, agree with what they say and then talk to each other about *our* way. To remind yourselves. He says this is a direct order that the Yanks of course don't have to obey. He doesn't know if you can get away with it, Cousins. I can order my men to sign. They're obeying a direct order. That isn't treason. I only wish I had a captain here to order *me* to sign. He says this to our lads—direct order: Form up at Sergeant-Major Fox's command and march with your heads up and sign the bastard paper on the bastard dotted line. Direct order, he says. He wishes you all the fucking very best. Form up.

And Fox marched them out. They enlisted as Peace Fighters. It wasn't to be easy, either. Each man was interrogated after every seminar. Every man had to write his autobiography, political and personal, and he was questioned. Liars were beaten and tortured, some died. Every man was held responsible for integrating his autobiographical narrative with his political course of study. Corporal Santore lived among them—they had floors and walls and, occasionally, old medicine—and he asked leading questions, he reported on the answers he got. Men who beat him, and there were several, were beaten by guards. Lies to my father had to be fitted to lies they told the interrogators. Few men, ill as they were, could remember the details of their stories, or what they had set down in their autobiographies. A lot of men were hanged by the hands because of my father. A number of them died. And when they marched out to enlist as Peace Fighters and survive another day, Lieutenant Pennels lay in the cave. He refused to come out. A detail of guards went in to persuade him to join his men. I suppose they kicked him to death. My father was with them. I can't believe he put the boot to him. I can't be responsible for him. I cannot ask him to answer to me. But I'd like to know. Perhaps he stood and watched. Perhaps he wept. I wonder what he said before he died. I meant

Lieutenant Pennels. I meant my father, too. Poor fathers. They are always asked these hard questions. "Are the rations good? What do you think of our folkways?" Hilary asked in the voice of the Chinese officer.

"Come on, smile for us, and that's the end of the story. Our hero chose how to die and that was that. And your father didn't do it, and you surely didn't do it."

"Do what?"

"Whatever was done. And now you know. And you needn't hear it from Fox."

"I knew most of it, Hilary. Regimental histories, American accounts of the camp. I knew your father ordered his men out. He saved them. He saved a lot of them."

Hilary said, with slow, cold anger, "He could have come out with them."

"Well."

"Yes, he could."

I looked at her narrow, handsome face, her patrician nose, the curly hair at her temples, the long neck and deep chest. I loved her for what she had told me.

She looked down her torso to me and said, "Let's show you off at the shop, shall we?"

"Stay here," I said. "Hilary."

"Let's go down to the shop, Peter. Please."

I climbed up, on the soft mattress, over the pillow that I'd disarranged, and over my own shirt that she lay back in, and then through it. I tore my own buttons from her, and then the cloth too. She didn't fight, she didn't embrace me, and she didn't quite lie passively either. Her hands went to my shoulders and gently lay there, as if I were tender with her and was someone she could trust. Except I was tearing at my clothes on her, and then was tearing at her, and her long strong arms lay delicately at either side of my neck, and my face was in her throat, her breasts, the hard armor of her breastbone. I couldn't name the sounds I made, but I heard the greedy, needful noises of a child as we fought, but didn't really fight, and made our love, but didn't really, and came at one another in our separateness and need. I didn't roll away. I was afraid to. I didn't want her to flee.

We were quiet for a long while. We almost slept. And then my face came up, though I didn't look at her. My face came up with its eyes closed and my mouth said, "I'm sorry. The story you were—"

She said, "I'm a tradeswoman, dear. This is a morning for business, and we're late. And you're too old for stories." In Fox's voice she said, "Off to work, laddie."

*S*alisbury was, I suppose, like the rest of England: changed, refusing change, old and new at once. I found it confusing and pretty. We passed a raw red brick shopping mall. We passed streets six hundred years old. At a long stone building that turned out to be a pub—it seemed to be part of a wall (it turned out that the wall enclosed the Cathedral)—I said, "Pretty building."

Hilary, parking the Range Rover, turned the ignition off and said, "Pretty? What sort of word is *that?*"

I gestured at the small shops across the street, the high amber stones of the Hart Inn beside us, the narrow street that in its shadows and turns seemed very old, sheltered from what made buildings new. "That. This. It's pretty. I like looking at it. That kind of pretty. What's wrong with pretty?"

Hilary was wearing black cowboy boots with high heels and a long tan crushed cotton skirt, a long-sleeved blue shirt with puffy shoulders, and a tight wide blue leather belt about her waist. Her hair was pulled back, and she looked older, efficient, impatient. She wore more make-up at the cheeks and eyes, I noticed. Even her voice sounded different; she might have been a newswoman on television, a shrew in a print shop on Southampton Road in London. She said, "Pretty somehow doesn't seem to adequately, you know, sum up a thirteenth-century city. Does it?"

70

"What's the next question, Hilary?"

"Pardon?"

"In the test. Or should I say examination."

"Oh, Peter. *Peter*. I did sound like a fussy bitch, didn't I? I sounded like a funny story about Englishwomen. Except it wasn't funny. Peter: I apologize. Forgive me. Forgive me. It was—it was getting dressed up for work and parking where I usually do. I thought for a moment I was alone. I think I resented *not* being alone. I'm quite used to being without people, you see. And I do like that, really. And you're changing things for me, aren't you? Not that I'm not helping you do it. I felt—competent, that's all. Now I belong to you again. Do you see?"

"You don't belong to me, Hilary."

"I want to, I think. Possibly maybe."

"Well, be sure."

"Peter, now you're the one sounds hesitant."

"I move that we stop talking."

She paused only a second before she said, "Second the motion."

"Passed," I said.

The sky had dropped lower, rain clouds hung above the city, and I wanted to stand outside the narrow entrance to the close near her shop and see if the heavy, dirty clouds impaled themselves on the high tan spire. The city felt cold and suddenly sad. "A goose just walked on your grave," Hilary said, watching me carefully.

On the corner outside her shop, and across the street from a tea shop, I slowly ran my hand up the back of her skirt and cupped a buttock and squeezed. "That's a goose,"

I said, pleased that she snorted and blushed and, blushing, led me past small tables of cheap used books and into the dark store. It smelled of cigarettes, of years of stale tobacco, strong and dark, that hung on the golden oak shelves that ran from the wooden floor to the high ceiling. The store was essentially a fairly wide corridor that went from the front door to a desk halfway down it, and then into a small back room with worktables on either side of the corridor; only a maroon curtain, now open, separated that room from the rest of the shop. In the front, where we stood, to the right and to the left, were the shelves. There were spines of cloth and leather and paper, and all stood neatly. On the floor and on small tables, on the lips of broad shelves and on the sills of the store windows, were stacked other books. The worktables in the back were littered with books and wrappers and book-mailing bags. And standing in the back room, watching us, her eyebrows raised like quotation marks around the word "lovers" on a printed page, was the woman Hilary called Florence. In the bright light of the surprisingly efficient fluorescent lamps she looked startled, bemused. She moved only to remove her cigarette, and then to put it to her mouth. She watched us.

"Peter Santore, Florence Pinkett. Flo, this is Peter. He's my friend from America."

"I never heard of you," she said. Her voice was harsh from cigarettes, and it reminded me of Fox's. "To be truthful, now, I did hear of you, but it was yesterday, teatime. Leicester rang and spoke of you at some length. He was somewhat pissed. Said you were youthful and inexperienced. You don't look all that young to me. And with her standing there red as sunset, I can't imagine you're inexperienced now, if ever you were."

Hilary said, "You're fired, Flo. Last check. Leave. Get out."

Flo said to me, "She does this once a week."

Hilary said, "I might mean it one day."

"I'll know it before you do," Flo said. "I'll be out before you come in, not to worry about that." She put her wet cigarette end into an ashtray and reached to a salad bowl on the worktable beside her. It was filled with packets of Rothman's cigarettes and, coughing, she began to open one. She said, "The lad in Dorchester who's always failing has failed. He's selling all his stock. Merriman of Dorchester Old Tomes rang up to gossip. And he can offer us *Tono-Bungay*, foxed endpapers, otherwise excellent, at only thirteen guineas over its value. I told him a tentative get-stuffed but said you'd probably fall for it in a day or two. And the mad woman with the alleged first-edition *Wuthering Heights* would, as usual, like you to call on her at your early convenience. And I'm going to brew some tea and fill the odd order if I'm not still fired and if you and he will excuse me."

Florence sat down, flicked on a hotplate, picked up a sheaf of papers, and ignored us. Hilary said, "Florence, I wonder if you'd mind taking care of the orders in this morning's post. Please feel free to have a cup of tea and relax as you do so. I shall return in half an hour, and then we can talk about the Wells. I may be cruel to Merriman."

"You will be," she said, looking at the papers. "You always are." She looked up, then, but at me. "Fox said you had a lot to learn."

"No jokes about me teaching him," Hilary warned, her voice low.

"I was only going to say that Fox also said you seemed determined to learn what you had to. Fox knows people."

In Fox's voice, Hilary said, "And people knows him."

Florence started. She said, "Don't *do* that."

We left her in the smoke and bright light of the back of the shop. I waved, but she wasn't looking. Hilary led me across the street and into the tea shop and sat, heavily, angrily. "She infuriates me. With her dank, dirty hair and her dirty jumpers and her bloody British women's walking shoes. It's like running some shop in London for lesbian literature. Did you see how she needs a shave? I think she uses Fox's electric shaver twice a week."

"She's Fox's wife?"

"She doesn't really use his shaver. Doesn't live with him. I'm not being fair. They're friends. She's the sister of a man Fox knew in the service. Dead. All of Fox's friends are dead, except me and Flo and some types who hang about in modern tacky bars and try to act young. They're friends, though. When he gets squiffed, she feeds him tea and eggs and greasy chips and calms him down. I hired her because of him, and I can't fire her because of him. But she's cheap. And she's very good. I even like her when the wind's right."

We drank coffee, and Hilary ate an enormous bun stuck full of slivered almonds and covered with honey. She watched me watch her slowly stick a finger deep into her mouth and suck off the sweetness. She pulled the finger out and looked at it, then me.

"Aren't I a proper tart," she said. Then she sat up, she wiped her hands on her napkin, and she said, "While I work to earn your keep, why don't you visit the cathedral? The biggest dumb blonde in the world. Henry James called her that."

Hilary kissed me goodbye, a soft, quick, casual kiss, and I walked down a cobbled street along a high stone wall until I found a way into the close. The cathedral was crowded with people who looked like me and people who didn't want to look like me, and people I didn't want to look like. People milled and talked too loudly and bought postcards. It was dim and huge, and I kept looking at the stone sarcophagi with the buried knights carved on top in bas-relief. Their legs were crossed at the ankle. They might lie in their armor, according to the carvings, and clutch their sword. None clutched his wife, though she, often enough, lay at least in bas-relief beside him on the stone; she was always smaller than he, and that difference in size made them look more separate. Words were carved on the flags of the floor, and, kneeling, I came to realize I walked on the names of the dead—that they lay beneath me, while the church climbed heavily above us toward heaven. I wanted to walk on my toes, to leap in the air and stay there so as not to be stepping on the dead. Around me lay the great raised coffins of heroes.

I left by a door that took me through a small cloister, and a quiet grassy lawn the Germans and Americans and Japanese had not discovered—this busload, at least—and in a kind of panic, fleeing heroes and a floor held up by bones, I was out behind the cathedral on a windy day, sun appearing and then hiding, clouds massing around the spire, great shadows turning the meadow I was in, which was rambled through by a small noisy stream, quite cold. I turned my back to the church and followed a gravel path, which in turn followed the stream, more or less, and soon I was in absolutely strange countryside, flat and dark, then flat and bright, then dark again with shadow, chilly and warm alternately, populated by cattle who didn't care, and by me. When I did look back at the cathedral, it looked familiar—not the church itself, but the way it looked, broader than I'd thought of it, and higher than I'd imagined, and somehow, in relation to where I stood, something I'd seen before.

On a bench overlooking the water, on the mossy faded wood that commemorated, according to its green metal plaque, a warden of the cathedral who had lived and died in its service, I sat with my hands folded on my lap and my head down on my chest. I heard birds that grunted and birds that sounded like flutes, and the water gurgled on rocks. I closed my eyes beneath the sounds as if they were a blanket I pulled up. Insects hung in the air about my face, and I imagined—dreamed?—that they became, with the noises of water and birds, the wind across trees and my own ears, a kind of screen. Inside it, on my face like the occasional heat of the sporadically unhindered sun, happily hot, was the present; beyond it, distant now, were Fox and his facts—what I'd sought, or sought to deal with, and which I'd now give much to forget. I forgot, for an instant, even what I wanted to escape. I dreamed while awake, and what I dreamed of was nothing. I heard the trees in the wind, I heard ducks, I thought, and yet I thought nothing. I was unconscious, and conscious of the fact.

And then I woke on the bench, slumped over, leaning on its iron arm, uncomfortable, grateful, chilled because the sun was not only screened again by clouds, but low and westerly; the cathedral looked even more familiar now than before I'd slept. She returned to me—I'd slept that deeply, that long—with the force of a new idea. My stomach jumped, and I felt fourteen.

I swear I hadn't heard him, or seen him approach. Fox was a little behind and to the left of me, wiping at his eye, and looming. He wore a dark blue blazer with silver buttons, and dark gray, almost black, sharkskin trousers. His shoes were aviator boots—he always looked as though he might pick up a sidearm and go into action. "Your hotel," he said.

"What?"

"That's quite like the Constable hanging near the lifts in your hotel."

"In my hotel in London," I said.

"Precisely."

"You're right. Now that you mention it. The same dark greens, and the stream—it looks wider in the painting. And of course the cathedral, just kind of, well, hanging there."

"Kind of hanging there," he echoed, imitating some American's speech, maybe mine. It was as aggressive a state-

ment as if he belched in my face from between those awful
teeth, or made a face to imitate mine, knowing that I'd
know it.

"I never told you where I was staying," I said.

"Of course you did. How are you this morning—well,
afternoon, really, isn't it. Have a late night, did you? Late
start this morning?"

"Mister Fox—"

"Why not call me Sergeant?"

"Because I'm not in the army. Did you drive down to
London—"

"Up. Up to London."

"I mean—why would you go looking for my hotel? I
couldn't have told you. I know I didn't. Hilary must have
mentioned it."

He nodded. He smiled. It was no smile.

"So you know it? Or you went back there?"

He said, "You dropped this." He handed me a leather-
bound notebook I often carry on trips. I make notations in
it, then later make full memoranda for our typists at the
office. I had left it in my larger suitcase, in the closet of
my hotel.

"In London," I said.

He shrugged, took his hand out of his blazer pocket, and
gestured at the cathedral while, with his other hand, he
wiped his eye. He'd delivered his warning: I was accessible,
a target, and he was a commando. "This is England," he
said. "This is why men died in wars."

I said, "Or why they ran away from them."

He nodded, as if to tell me how much he'd been expect-

ing such a celebration of cowardice from the son of a cele-
brated coward. I saw Hilary walking toward us beside the
river. She stopped to throw something toward the ducks
and geese, and they surrounded her. I wanted to look at her
and not speak, and maybe Fox did too. He was silent for
ten or fifteen seconds, anyway; I could feel him looking at
her. "She's my responsibility," he said.

"I'm sure her father would be grateful."

"Oh, don't patronize me, my young American boy. Did
you serve in your so-called peacetime army? Did you lie
and cheat so you could find your youthful way into Vietnam? I'm a *soldier*."

"Well, fuck it, Fox. I never said you weren't. Why'd
you go to London, or come out here? To—to persecute
me. I never did a goddamned thing to you. I came here—"

"Yes?"

"I'm here with Hilary. She wants me to be. Butt out."

"Young Peter, you sound like an American joke. *Butt
out*. I think the villain chap in the film you think you're in,
and of course I never mind playing the role of the villain
chap—what else are Sergeant-Majors for? He'd say to you,
'Who's gonna make me?' Am I right? Now, you have, as
Americans here keep telling us, as if we mightn't without
their permission, you have a real good day."

He strode, marched, dammit, with swinging arms, down
the gravel walk toward Hilary. I watched her stop as he
approached. I saw her drop the bread or whatever she'd
been feeding the ducks. They crowded in on her to eat.
Her shoulders drooped, her neck leaned forward, and she
was subject to Fox again: his.

They stayed that way a while, as Fox talked and Hilary nodded, he tall and broad above her, she slumped and small-looking. She chatted a bit, even smiled; when she did, I did, I realized. So there was plenty to worry about, in case anyone wondered if my autumn vacation was suitably free of woe. And then he released her, and she walked toward me, straightening as she came. Crows or choughs or some damned black birds were diving toward trees near the river, and the ducks and geese cackled and called as she walked, swinging her bag and showing her teeth.

She didn't stop until she was against me, chest on chest and thigh on thigh; I hugged her for balance as well as to feel her and then to be saying hello.

We turned and walked away from the cathedral, not speaking. The ducks waddled after us for a while, and then gave up. I said, "Did you know that my hotel has a painting of this?"

"This what?"

"This meadow. The field here, with the church behind us."

"Oh, it must be one of the Constables. He painted here, where we're walking. What a lovely painter, don't you think?"

"Do you know the painting I mean?"

"Why, Peter?"

We slowed but kept walking, and I said, "Hilary, why are we together?"

Without hesitation she answered, "For my part, you're a very good lay, and you spend lots of money on me, and for a lawyer you're astonishingly innocent. And there's a reasonably good chance I'm falling in love with you and your dirty blue shirts and your sad face."

"Well, I myself have been hating it. I like to do it every once in a while for charity. You know, like the Lend-Lease Program."

"I hope I've shown myself to be suitably grateful," she said.

"I want to stop joking now, Hilary."

She stopped. "All right." She stood back. "But don't tell me, please, that you don't care for me. I won't ask how much, but you must be caring for me."

I stepped in and kissed her. This wasn't one of those husbandly I'll-see-you-later kisses, either, and we knew it and grew breathless.

"Why don't we hate each other, Hilary?"

Her face twisted. "That's such a stupid question, Peter! Because your father chose the way he wanted to live and die? Because our hero did? You mean they own us from the bloody *grave?*"

I thought of Fox, but thought to not speak of him. I thought, in fact, to stop thinking. I felt as though, that moment, as the field grew warm again, and as the pattern of the shadows on us changed, that the spire of Salisbury Cathedral was a giant sundial, and we were numbers, and the long dark arm had fallen upon us. We were the hour silently tolled. I didn't want to think that. And Hilary, whom I'd sought with a head stuffed and humming like a tenement of hives, was now my way of escape. I held her, then hugged her, then strained at her, so that our kiss grew too intense for us to stay on our feet. We were swaying, and about to fall.

She pushed back a little and breathed on my face. She smelled like last night, and I moved to go back for more.

"Peter, English girls don't do it in the fields in sight of Salisbury Cathedral anymore. Not since the end of the last century, dear. Hotels, laddie. Lovely, anonymous hotels. Come on." She took my hand in both of hers, I paused to pick up her bag, and we walked rather quickly through the shadows and the noisy ducks toward the close, and then the Red Lion. I looked back to see what time the spire had cast, but the clouds blowing in had laid a dozen giant stripes on the meadow. Hilary said, "I like the way you answer, Peter."

"What was the question, again?"

"Never mind," she said.

So we did go up to my room and make love. I bit at her thighs and belly. She buried her face in my neck. We were trying to hide. Afterward, as we drove in her Rover out on the A30 toward the Golden Pheasant, she turned periodically to look at me. And once, I saw, she shook her head and smiled.

"What was that for?" I asked.

"I was considering, if you must know, having a kind of little orgasm while I shifted up from fourth."

I put my hand on her stomach and cupped it. She shivered, and I felt as though I'd won a difficult case. Men *are* such pigs, I thought, helplessly grinning.

The Golden Pheasant was the sort of place you go to England to sit in with women like Hilary Pennels. The ceiling was low, with dark joists showing, and the walls were a creamy plaster. People with round red faces drank bitter, or that awful English invention, lager with Rose's lime juice, or—as I did—double whiskeys, and there was no music, but loud talk. We had snacks of game pie with a nasty red wine, and then I went back to whiskey and Hilary to the nursing of a small gin. She chatted with the barmaid, who was dressed like an executive vice-president of something profitable, and she introduced me to a wealthy farmer and a man who had just quit his job; he was being toasted, repeatedly, and we joined in the toasts. It was warm, and we'd all grown sweaty and boisterous, disheveled. The man who had quit his job—he'd been a chemist with some international giant—stood on his stumpy legs and wobbled at the bar. He raised his jar of bitter and, blinking his dark eyes, smoothing at the seven or eight hairs he'd brushed across his forehead, rubbing his five o'clock shadow, and trying to pull at the necktie he'd long before discarded, he made his speech. "Ladies and gentlemen, and acquaintances old and new. It gives me great pleasure to announce the end of my life—I mean career—and the start of something fresh."

"A bloody ripping great hangover," someone shouted, and everyone laughed.

"That too, my fellow inebriate, that too. But I should be remiss if I were not to mention those whose departure has made it impossible for me to consult with them before taking this small but important step toward independence in my fiftieth year. So, as I think of those who in my life have guided me—"

"You'll be talking all night," the wag interrupted. "We'll *never* get to drink."

"Quite right," the toaster said. "Quite right. Although I did want to mention mum and dad."

"And everyone else you knew from the age of two. Get on with it, old dear."

He smoothed his hair. He searched for the knot of his tie. I knew what he was going to say. He said, "Without further ado, then. Ladies, gentlemen, I give you: Those gone on—though out of sight we recognize them with our glasses."

Hilary sighed and sighed and sighed; it was like listening to air that slowly leaked from a tire. It went on and on. I looked at her hands—they were cupped around her glass of gin. Then I looked at her face, and saw how its muscles gripped her expression, held it together, as tightly as her fingers wound at the gin.

"Let's leave," I said.

"You know, I'm afraid I've already left, Peter."

I nodded at her as she nodded at me, and we smiled at each other, but carefully, as you smile at someone who's ill and would rather you not discuss it.

The night was clear as we drove up the narrow road that went to Hilary's. When I looked behind us, I thought that I could see each light on the Salisbury Plain.

"You should read *The Return of the Native*," she said. "He describes what you're seeing so well."

"But I'm seeing it."

"Imagine what you'd see after you saw it through Thomas Hardy's eyes."

"Thomas Hardy again. Stonehenge and fate and raped while asleep."

"It is everybody's fate to be raped while asleep."

"And what in Christ does *that* mean, Hilary?"

"I'll be buggered if I know."

"And in your sleep."

"No, thank you. And never mind. And sorry. I was getting gloomy. Here we are. Home. Well: home to me."

"It feels homey to me too."

"When do you have to go to *your* home, Peter?"

"When—I don't know."

"When you get what you've come here for, you were going to say. And could you tell me what that is?"

"I couldn't tell myself, much less you. It has—it had to do with you."

We'd gone inside and were making tea—instant coffee for me—and Hilary was coming downstairs in jeans and a kind of oatmeal-textured sweater. In the living room, the sitting room as she called it, we sat together on the lumpy sofa and sipped.

"All right, then," she said. "If you can't tell yourself what you want, and you can't tell me, can you tell us what you *thought* you were after when you flew here in the first place?"

I took a sip. I took a breath. I said, "You."

She put her cup down while looking at me. She said, "That's what I'd thought. Did you come here to fuck your way into my brain? It's the long way round to the head, I should think."

I reached for her hand and brought it to my lips and kissed it. She opened her palm on my mouth, then slid it onto my cheek, and then over my ear until her fingers were buried in my hair. And then she bared her teeth as she gripped my hair and pulled, yanked, drove my face down toward the tea tray, up again, then down. "This is getting dangerous for me," she seethed through gritted teeth. "Tell me. I'm losing—I—*tell*."

I didn't pull away. The pain had brought tears to my eyes, and I wiped at them. I thought, of course, of Fox. She was crying. I remember thinking, *Hilary's crying too.* Because I was, also, and my tears hadn't all that much to do with my pulled hair or the scratches her nails had made on my scalp.

She sat back, looking at me. She shook her head, and I shook mine.

"Hilary," I said. "I didn't know what I was after. I'd written to—Jesus, everyone in your father's outfit. Everyone. All the way up to the regimental headquarters, the Ministry of Defence, retired senior officers. I've got a file in my office bigger than I'd put together for a criminal defense. Maybe that's what I was putting together. I don't know. I found out where you lived. I wrote to a firm in London we do some business with, and I asked for a briefing on you. They checked with someone here, in Salisbury—I don't remember the firm. I have their name in my suitcase."

"Someone spied on me? Somebody I know?"

I shook my head. "It's the kind of thing—it's less of a fuss than a credit check. No, nobody came lurking and snooping, none of that. I just wanted to know who survived your father and where his family lived, and it came up you. Hilary Pennels, Summerslow, near Salisbury, Wiltshire, England. So I took my vacation time and I came here. I was going to stay in the Red Lion and look for you."

"You didn't come upon Fox and me by calculation, then."

"By sandwiches and a terrific bottle of wine, Hilary. By accident."

"There are no accidents. Read Hardy."

"Hilary, I wasn't there to *spy*. I would have found you, because I don't get tired of looking for things, and I would have driven up here in my little rented car, and I'd have knocked at the door and—"

Her fingers tightened in my hair. "And *what?*" She stood, and she put her other hand on the other side of my head. She crouched above me, saliva gleaming on her teeth, her mouth looking bruised, her face dead white. "*What?*" she shouted, whipping my head back and forth, side to side, back and again, back and again. I put my hands on her wrists and came out of the chair and onto my knees. My head slammed into the floor, and then the momentum of her shaking picked me up again, so that I was back on my knees, hands on her forearms, face burning, scalp bloody, eyes filled with tears.

"To find out what I owed you. To find out if I—*owed* you anything."

"Money?"

"Of course not. Trust me, Hilary."

"*Trust* you? I spread my legs for you. I wrapped them around your lanky American back. I *loved* you."

What I said then was everything I'd thought not to say to her, or anyone I knew: "Don't stop."

She gripped my hair as if she were going to hurl my head into the fireplace behind us. Then she was on her knees before me, panting, weeping, hissing at me: "Bastard. Yankee son of a bitch bastard. You *betrayed* me."

"How?"

"Oh, don't come the lawyer with me now, Peter. This isn't a courtroom. You were a spy in my house."

"Hilary, like my father?"

I'd calculated that one, and it stopped her, as I'd thought it might. Because she shook her head. "I'm sorry," she said. "No."

"Yes, I am, goddamnit. Don't tell me when I'm sorry and when I'm not. That's what fucking Fox does. You be you. Let me be me. And I am sorry. Because I don't want to tar you with your father. We have a right, both of us, to live our own lives. Which is what I was trying to do when you decided to infiltrate mine. But I wasn't meaning it as if— you and he, you know. You have to understand that, certainly."

"I came here to see if the obligation—no: I don't know. Hilary, I think maybe my father helped kill yours."

"I expect he did, in a way," she said. Her legs were out behind her, parallel to one another, and she propped herself on one arm, as if she were at a picnic. She had stopped looking at my face. I put my hand into my hair, and my fingertips looked bloody when I pulled them away from my scalp. My face and head burned, and I was surprised to find that the pain made me glad. "But you aren't responsible for what your father did."

"Not legally," I said.

"Not in any way. No. Let's say this, Peter, once and for all. You do not owe me anything, moral, spiritual, psychological, emotional, or financial. Is that what you came here for?"

"Not what I'm here for now, though."

"Now you're here for me."

"Yes."

"You're enchanted with me."

"Yes."

"You're taken with me."

"Yes."

"Infatuated."

"Yes."

"But more."

"Yes."

"You love me, Peter."

"Yes."

"Peter: you love me?"

"Yes."

"Shouldn't you be asking the questions and I the one who's answering them? Isn't that your work?"

"Yes."

"You defend people guilty of crimes."

"Yes. No. Accused of them."

"But some of them are guilty."

"Yes."

"And are you here, I don't know, to somehow defend your father?"

"No."

"Because it would be all right if you needed that."

"No."

"You only came to see if you had—obligations to me."

"That's right."

"And I've told you that you don't. But, Peter: have you considered whether you came here to see if it is *you* who are owed anything? Pardon, or, I don't know—forgiveness will do."

"Hilary, I'm making my peace with him. Isn't that what—"

"War," she said.

"Pardon?"

"You're making war. Don't you think I know? You're really in a war with him. Our hero, after all, declared his war on me, just as your great traitor did on you. Your bastard chose to come home, at least. Our hero, don't you forget—I don't—chose to leave my mother and me. His men, his war, his honor, his—any other little word all full of pus and blood and body gas and emptiness. You name it. His fucking *heroism*. That was more important than we were. You see, he abandoned us. I've been so angry with him, every moment, ever since I learned that. It's what he left me, his legacy. War. You too, Peter. The hero chose his route, the traitor his, and their paths crossed. And then ours did. And then you fell in love with me. Say that."

"I fell in love with you."

"And it's true."

"And it's true."

"No! You *bloody* stupid man! *Tell* me if it's true."

"It's true."

"So we're not fucking Romeo and Juliet, are we? Or anybody else who's doomed not to love each other? Because you know that I love you."

"Of course. That's why you tore my hair out."

"I was working to get at *your* brain. I'd tried the indirect route, and now I was working at something with a bit more immediacy to it. Could we kiss each other?"

I leaned over, still on my knees, and she leaned up, and only our lips touched. It was a long, soft, delicate kiss, and in the middle of it, Hilary began to cry.

She patted my face, gently, and she stood up and went to the mantel and took down a book. The jacket had a woodcut on it, and of course it was *Tess of the D'Urbervilles*. Inside, on the title page, Hilary had written *Fate, Peter*.

I said, "It probably is, don't you think?"

She didn't answer. She left the room. There was silence. And then she called, from the stairs, "I'm going to bed. I'm falling asleep right away. I want to find out if you really can be raped in your sleep."

Early the next morning, I drove the Escort back to Salisbury and the Red Lion. I was in town before the morning's traffic had begun. In the streets around the hotel, in the cool cloudy parchment-colored light, I had a sense of what this market town might have been in Thomas Hardy's day. I carried his book upstairs to my room. I took a very long bath, and changed my clothes, made arrangements for cleaning the clothes I'd been wearing and, downstairs, sitting over coffee and sausage and biscuits and eggs, I sent postcards to the office, to one or two friends, and of course to Bert and my mother. The photo on the card was of the old courtyard at the Red Lion, outside the stables where now the patrons parked their cars. *Dear Bert and Mom,* I wrote, *The bed is two hundred years old. The sheets are newer. Much love—*

In jeans and desert boots, with a cardigan sweater I'd bought in London in the shop of my posh hotel, I went out with *Tess of the D'Urbervilles* and ended up reading on the lawn, inside the cathedral close. Every time I looked up, the spire had changed in the light; I liked it best when I could see how brown it was, and thick, not delicate as in drawings, but heavy and sturdy, a serious piece of business done by men who respected themselves. It didn't look like any dumb blonde to me. But, then, there were good reasons I didn't spend my recreational hours with Henry James.

And yet here I was with Hardy, and a chapter about a man engrossed in working back to find his roots. Well, there was more to it, of course, but I felt sympathetic to the foolish guy because he was thirsty for his history, for somehow dealing with it; so was I. I didn't want money, though, or rank, anything better than the hand that I'd been dealt. I wasn't after advantage, was I? It was a question I still couldn't answer. My scalp tingled as I thought of trying to answer it.

You can't be raped in your sleep, I told Tess, as she wandered up to the manor house and, clearly, the start of all her troubles. No: Hilary would say that her troubles had started with her birth. I thought of her, and with every tentative step of Tess's, each crimson-faced difficulty, I thought of her more. We were to meet for lunch, but it was only almost ten, and I kept hearing her breath as she whipped her head back and forth against the sheets. So I mailed my cards, and I drove the Escort back up the A30, then Hilary's winding road.

When I'd read a bit of Tess's story, I'd called to her, in my imagination, *Go back!* It seemed like a novel much concerned with footsteps—where people walked, and where they ventured forth when they could have turned around. *Go back*, I'd thought to advise her. And when I saw Fox's teal-colored Mini, all rusted and dented and scratched, looking as though he had hurled it through bushes and forest and—who knows?—people standing in his way, I gave the same advice to myself.

As is so often the case with people who give advice professionally, especially lawyers, I ignored the wisdom I'd have insisted on anyone else. It was a lovely day, and I was falling in love, or was already in it, or in its neighborhood, my brains were in my cock and balls and blood, and I was not about to turn around. I went out back, and though their coffee cups were on the table, and the chairs were shoved away from its edge, Fox and Hilary weren't there. I knocked at the back door, then went around to the side. I banged on it, and nobody came. I went in. I loved the feeling that I ought to. For, as a lawyer, knowing what I did about property, I'd showed myself, by turning the knob, that I refused to think of Hilary and me as separate. My mother lived in her separate life in a separate state of the Union, and in a sense—her past had roared inside her in my boyhood like a storm, I think—she always had; my father had declared himself a citizen of anyplace but where I lived. And I, through all my years of growing up, and all the cases of my practice, and all the small, saddening love affairs I'd carried clumsily from uneasy start to broken finish, I had always lived alone. And suddenly I was in another country, in someone else's house, all but breaking-and-entering, as I had broken-and-entered her life. Because I had wanted to find we were the same, perhaps. Because, maybe, I'd become exhausted by living so profoundly alone. Seeking a sister-in-history, even if she lived at the opposite pole of our shared experience, I had found a person who thought, I thought, to live inside my skin, and who seemed to be inviting me to live inside of hers. So I think that I could not have obeyed such useful words as *Go back*. That, I am convinced, is why we're given choice at such moments: to always make the wrong one.

As I came up the curling, narrow, creaking wooden stairs from the empty downstairs rooms I had walked through, I heard a funny voice. It was Hilary's, I would have sworn, her rich, husky voice, but it also was not. I'd never heard it, I thought, but it sounded familiar. It sounded, in fact, like mine. And that's what it was. It came from Hilary's bedroom, and if you'd heard me once or twice, you would have said that Peter Santore was talking from inside an Englishwoman's bedroom, and maybe from under Mary Louise's and Martha's knots.

"The thing is," I heard me say, "I don't really know what he wanted a doo. Ya know? Maybe he wanted a come home. He wasn't such a grown-up guy, I mean. He was a kid. He hadda be confused, unnerstan? His motha, my grandmotha, she died a long time ago. Well, she was a wop. A dago, ya know? His fatha wasn't. He was half some kinda Indian. Really. Onondaga Indian. You put that togetha, the kid's gonna be confused. His motha made him grow up a Are-See. His old man died. Get this. In prison—Jamesville. Yeah. Ya like that foah iyanee? The kid musta always been ashamed. That's what my motha useta tell me. Befoah she stopped talkin about im. Ya think it's enough, that kinda life, to turn a kid ina that kinda rebel? That kinda traita?" Then I paused in my remarkable soliloquy, which permitted me to think about what I hadn't quite said to her all at once, but which she'd assembled from days and nights, hours, minutes, passing remarks and half-asked questions. Whatever she was, a part of my brain did manage to make me understand, she was sympathetic somehow, and a wonderful listener, attentive, retentive, brilliant.

I went on: "Nah. I just can't buy it. Whateveh was on his mind. I—ya gotta be a real shit to do what he did. Ya gotta be a fuckin *outlaw*. Ya break the law, or ya don't. Ya fathuh wooden, even to live. My fatha helped kill yaw fathuh just for goddam *food*."

And then Fox, as if speaking in argument, said, "Yes, old thing, but the chap would have to eat in order to live. Don't you see?"

And Hilary, coughing, no doubt from the strain of ventriloquizing so long, said, "But, Fox. I thought we hated Peter's father. Well, I actually don't. I know you do, though."

"Always try to be fair, sweet girl. Even to one's enemies."

"I doan wanna be yoah enemy," I said in Hilary's mouth.

"I don't want him to be our enemy," said Hilary in her own voice.

"Speak for yourself. Act for yourself. You're your own person, aren't you?" Fox said. I heard the rustle of bedclothes I knew well. I heard familiar bedsprings whine familiarly. I heard the sound of flesh on flesh—as if he'd struck her, for his next words were, "Didn't I ask you a question, girl? Hilary?"

"Yes." It was low, as if she looked down, or were facedown in bed.

"And did you answer me?"

"No."

"Why not?" He sounded surprised. No: he sounded as though, in a ritual way they knew to speak, he was supposed, now, to sound as if surprised. "Why not, Hilary?"

"Stubborn," she said. "Naughty. Bad."

"That's right."

"Naughty—Fox. Fox?" Her voice shifted tones, it was lower, now, the voice I knew as always hers. Nothing, I guess, was always hers. "Fox," she said, "I don't want to do this."

"Oh," he said. "Well, that's all right. You do it anyway."

"Fox."

"I'll fill you full of lead if you don't. You will *not* betray me."

"Peter," she said. She was telling him my name, saying her other loyalty or treason, but I felt summoned by her. The door before me, low and narrow, hanging on iron hinges and made of dark vertical planks, was the final door before me for the rest of my life. This—I knew it, absolutely, no matter how many I walked through after today—would be the last door to matter. I heard the bed move, but I could not: I was too exhausted to lift my hand, and my knees were close to trembling. This knowledge, the gift of this moment, the unbearable richness I might open into, would be another life from mine. I backed toward the stairs and went down. And I hardly knew, until I was on the road, that I'd come down the hill at too great a speed for second gear, and it wasn't until I was heading toward Salisbury that I noticed how the gear box smelled and smoked. I changed up, and drove faster.

On the A30, I heard Peter Santore say, in the voice in which I usually heard myself speak, "I didn't think I sounded like that." And so, of course, I started to laugh. I laughed the way you sneeze while driving at high speeds—arms straight out and hands clenched hard on the steering wheel, neck extended and face aimed high beyond the steering wheel's curve, barking explosions of laughter while trying, still, to see. By Stockbridge I'd declined into feeble giggles. And by Basingstoke, I'd nothing to hide in, not laughter, simperings, chuckles, or snorts of derision. I felt as though I carried a wound, something open and puckered and raw. I felt, outside Staines, as though the bullet or shrapnel were still inside me. I felt weak, as though I'd bled a lot. I felt as though the wound were beginning to rot. I had my other bag in London, and the bulk of my belongings. I could ask the Red Lion to ship my one valise, or, even better, I could leave it behind. Didn't a routed army leave the landscape behind it littered with its baggage and its dead? I would drive back to London and drop off the car and spend the night in the hotel, changing the bandage and pouring whiskey onto the wound, a time-honored procedure, I understood. And I would make the first flight out that had a seat for me. Salisbury was behind the lines. London was the frontier. Nobody told me *Go back* as I drove so dangerously, weaving and passing impatiently, reckless, wounded, and fleeing for my life.

In my hotel, I waited for the elevator in a small alcove with a wall composed of the Constable painting of the fields behind the close at Salisbury. It was an enormous, enlarged photograph, laminated and a little blurry—as if stretched in the enlarging, I now saw—with horses and cattle at a stream, and long black shadows reaching through the cruelly green meadows. I felt as if still pursued, and I felt weaker than before, as if my wound were bleeding. I dropped my clothing on the floor and crawled, but gingerly, under the sheet and blanket.

The pain grew worse, and I was in The Caves. I tried to think of the others, to hear them or to smell them, even, but I couldn't unless I forced the sensory image up like a prayer. I was bound inside myself. The self I was trapped in lay inside The Caves above the Thirty-eighth Parallel. They were very low—no European could stand inside them. They were so dark that one had to feel his way about by following the shallow icy rivers that welled from the back of the cave like blood, or by tracking one's way along the walls; they were thick with chalky matter, bat dung, I supposed, and they stank with a high, ammoniac bite at the sinuses. There was always the pain, which was deeper than ache or throb, because more was affected than a small concentration of nerves. The wound went back and down and in, as The Caves did. And of course there were the crawling things, whether lice or maggots in the rotten parts, or both. And bats flew low and brushed the flesh. And rats waded, large enough to make a trilling splash. The bowels blew gas and fecal blood in little spatters like a soft, polypy creature dying, and the knee- and elbow- and finger-joints swelled. There were moments when I was simply a thin-skinned balloon of foulnesses. I wept because I hated what I was.

You must only survive, I told myself. You must not consider the politics between the warring parties or within the smaller group. You must keep from putrefying, from choking in your own fluids, and from going into shock; you must not sleep until you find a dream that you won't die of; you must surely avoid, while you seal away the pain in a single cold glow in a corner of your body, the confrontation of what you will be tempted to examine as values. We are not weighing motives, I said to the pain when it tried to come from the wound through my shoulders and arms to my splayed fingers. We are not going to offer recriminations, or any sort of absolution, either. We are going to lie in this darkness we have come to, and we are going to breathe.

It was difficult, in the damp and chill and blind blackness, to skirt despair. The Chinese had a man outside the cave on a crucifix. He was a sergeant of American infantry who had been swept along in the retreat. They had beaten him on the march because after he had run out of ammunition for his .30-caliber carbine, he had turned the stubby gun around and had beaten at the Chinese soldiers surrounding him. He'd been a kind of baying dog, heaving his terror and rage from deep in his throat. He'd shattered the stock against the shoulder of an officer, whose collarbone had smashed. And they had beaten him with sticks on the march, more angry that he wouldn't die than that he'd hurt them. They knew, of course, that he would die soon enough, for they had fractured his jaw, and he couldn't eat or drink. The British had fashioned a straw for him, from reeds, but the captors had taken it. His face looked as though someone had split it in two at the nose, then put it back together very crookedly. It was swollen with blood and outraged tissue, and his eyes were black. And now he was hanging by the ankles from a crucifix, his legs spread and tied with thongs to the horizontal bar. His blood filled his face, forcing its weight at his broken jaws. He was trying to scream with pain, but of course he couldn't. He made the sound you would expect a man in agony to make through jaws that would not open. And each time he made it, the sound was not what you'd thought to expect.

All you had to do was join the Peace Fighters, and sign the petition against the war and the United Nations, and you would receive medical assistance. Someone would pluck the maggots from the open lips of your puckering wound. Someone would cut the gangrenous toes that stank, and someone would find you even aspirin, you'd been told. And your men would live, and you would live, and the war would be over, and you would go home to the cottage in Wiltshire, outside Salisbury, to your wife and your daughter. It was the Yank told you that, the fellow with the curious habit of lowering his head as though he ducked away from something behind him.

He was the one mentioned aspirin, and you laughed. He had the largest, darkest eyes—looked a Red Indian, as a matter of fact, and sounded sly, with his soft voice, his wit. He tried to make jokes, American jokes that no one in the jailers' squadron understood, and no one among the British. Kept talking about Abbot and Costello, and Amos 'n Andy. "Well, hello dere, Kingfish," he liked to say. An American prisoner tried to throttle him; he simply stood before him, his neck in the prisoner's frail paws, with his dark eyes closed. When they pulled the prisoner away from him, he said, so gently, "We are all on the side of those in thrall. We are all on the side of the worker. You and me. We're the bees. We're all the bees, buddy." He never came back without a North Korean soldier with a mounted bayonet. "Hello dere, Kingfish."

You held the lips of your wound together, and you came to the decision that you'd never see your daughter again. You told it to the Yank who had decided not to see his son. You and he were men discarding wives, and the babies they'd borne you. What the Yank and you were choosing was the absence men and women worked so hard to avoid.

I drank a lot of whiskey and it made me sleep, but not for long. I woke, it felt, shortly after I fell asleep. I drank more whiskey and I slept and woke and drank. I held the lips of the wound together, and wriggled against the lice and maggots and rats and the water like blood, and the blood that ran down into it, and the bats that screamed, or my screams against their leathery low circlings, and the sounds from the man upside down with the blood in his face and the jaws that would not let him say his pain.

Maybe the lieutenant and the Red Indian Yank knew that it all, anyway, was a matter of everyone leaving. Maybe they were the sort of men intended to leave. And maybe more of us left than remained, left by remaining. Maybe it was those who were not prisoners, and wounded, and deceitful, and always on their way away, who were the exception. I was not going to think about it, though, because I was buried in the darkness in the low, cold Caves at the border, on the edge. Goodbye. Bye-bye. Bye-bye.

One of the tricks the North Koreans hadn't used at first, but which the Chinese introduced, was the boxes into which the already broken men were folded and jammed. It wasn't the actual use of the box, or the breaking of bones and crushing of soft, frayed organs that the Chinese suggested; the North Koreans were clever enough for that on their own. No. It was a simple enough fillip. The Chinese, a musical people, liked to beat on the boxes with sticks. There were no melodies, no lyrics or variations, only the slow, rhythmic boom of the songs that sounded through the boxes into the spine and skull and of course through the ragged lips of the wound. The repeated thudding became for the men inside the sound of time itself, abstracted and refined, perfected. When they came outside, if they could walk again, and if they ever understood again what they were knowing, they found the world a silent place in which time grew slow and soggy, unmarked; the world, they discovered, was a place in which little happened except pain, and so slowly that a number of them swore that they were dead. Some of the parts of their bodies, their swollen balls especially, had burst when they were folded into the box. So they were, soon, as dead as they assumed.

It seemed that the Chinese were at it again. Except, of course, I wasn't bleeding into the boards of the box, but only onto the bed, in my London hotel. I wasn't concussed by the Peace Fighters' metronomes, but by my hangover. I didn't understand, quite, how I could be hung over while I still, so evidently, was drunk. I remember saying to myself, as I realized what I was going to do, "Well, I'm drunk. You can't blame *me*." While I was twisting at a light switch, and reading the instructions for directory assistance,

I was thinking, I remember, of Tess of the D'Urbervilles. I told her, and the telephone, "You *can* get raped in your sleep."

You can.

The operator sounded unfriendly, gruff, as if I'd wakened him. But he gave me the number for the cottage with the roof of living thatch. "Mind how ye go," I said, remembering what bobbies were alleged to say.

"You too," he sneered.

Of course I did visualize her lying under Fox when the phone rang to wake her. She repeated her number, gummily, foggily, sounding worried. And, before I could speak, her voice clarified. "Peter," she said.

"This," I announced, "is Peter."

"Yes."

"You expected me," I told her.

"I thought you might ring. Or come back. I was thinking, it might be more like you to come back."

"I'm not as much like me as I used to be."

"Oh, Peter."

"Put Fox on, please."

"He isn't here."

"Just checking." I'm afraid I snickered.

"There's nothing more for you to check on, Peter. Now you know everything. You found out the worst. I thought you'd come up my stairs to rescue me. It—"

"He was raping you in your sleep?"

"Peter."

"It was all against your will."

"Yes."

I said, "No."

"Peter!"

"No," I said.

The sound of the wires, of the long transmission of nothing, shushed out between us and back. I hugged myself, elbows close to my ribs, keeping the edges of the wound from opening out. She finally said, "No," very wearily.

So I in my wisdom repeated it. "No."

Then more of the shushing. It sounded like those old 78 records of sopranos from the Thirties that you sometimes hear on WQXR in New York on weekend afternoons—the loud silence that comes after the needle drops, and before she starts to celebrate her solitude.

"This is the saddest—"

I said, "You loved it. I heard your voice, remember. I heard your voices. You were doing a swell rendition of *me*."

She started to hiccup giggles. It was hysterical laughter, so who better to join in than Pete the prick? I laughed along with her, hearing my syllables swap with hers. And then we stopped, and then we listened for one another.

At last, Hilary said, "I was trying to persuade him to leave you alone."

"You were cajoling him," I said.

"Yes."

"Coaxing him."

"That's right."

"Lulling him, you could say."

"Peter."

"You keep on saying that, Hilary."

In a terrible whisper: "I don't know anything else I can say."

"Tell me."

"Peter: *what?*"

"The truth," the brilliant lawyer demanded. "Tell me the truth."

"Which one?"

"*What?*"

"About what, Peter? About why Fox wanted to hurt you?"

"Because of my father."

"Yes."

"And yours."

"Of course."

"I don't blame him," I said.

"Darling Peter," Hilary said, as if I weren't on the phone, as if she were writing me a letter on one of those folded blue aerograms they sell you. When she said it again, "Darling Peter," and when I thought again of the airmail form, I realized how soon I would be gone, and how far, and forever.

"So you were making believe to make fun of me," I said. "You had to burn the village to save it."

"What village?"

"And why were you lying spread-legged underneath a man so old he could—"

Her voice changed. It wasn't Fox's, or mine; it wasn't

the one of hers I'd grown used to. It was hard, and high—she spoke from her throat, no resonance of chest or stomach in her words—and she sounded as though she were panting. She said, "Finish it, Peter."

"No."

"Tell me about myself. I enjoy learning what I've become. Why I've become it. I come from a long line of variously roundheeled intellectuals and warriors. I've just wandered into being, sort of, a combination of the two. A soldier's crumpet. A sergeant-major's whore. With overtones, need we say, of school-leaver's fury, that sullen kind of lower-class anger you find riding next to you in nasty boots on the Underground. And a touch, would you say, of Kraft-Ebbing. His breath, you know, isn't as nasty as his teeth. He sucks on mints. Cloves, sometimes."

"Sometimes you," I apparently had to say. "When it wasn't *my* turn."

Her voice harshened, and spoke as Fox: "Well said, laddie."

"I'm sorry I came here, Hilary," I said, crying like someone thirty years younger.

Fox's voice said, "Times get rough, lad, a man holds onto his ballocks with one hand, his weapon with the other. Steady on." And then, promptly, she was Hilary again, the voice I was accustomed to, the one I'd heard in the storeroom of her cottage, on the bed at the Red Lion Inn. She said, "It isn't you."

"I came hunting you, Hilary. I would have used you, I think."

She said, "Peter, for *what?*" And then: "I know." And then: "You did." And she said, "You feel so betrayed. Dear boy—"

The wordless noise in the wires between us went on. I was lying in my bed, my eyes closed but smarting under the weight of the bedside lamp. I managed to click it off, and then in the darkness, with the telephone on my chest, my arms once more at my sides, clamped to staunch, I let my heavy lids slide down, and I listened.

"—and awfully soon. I mean, it's possible," she was saying, sounding young.

"I have to hang up, Hilary. Ring off. However you people say it. I have to get away from you. I'm going home. I have a flight tomorrow."

"When?"

"I don't know. I have to find one tomorrow. I—"

"Were you listening? Just now?"

"I'm falling asleep here, Hilary."

"When I was telling you about Fox?"

His name, I learned just then, was capable of starting up a heart half-eaten by dogs. My eyes in the darkness were wide. "What?" I said. "What?"

"He knows where your hotel is. He's been there."

"Goddamned right, he has."

"He might go back again."

"I'll leave tonight," I said, reminding myself of the difference between my father and hers. "Now."

"Yes," she said. She said, "I'll miss you all my life."

And as I opened my mouth to tell her what I had to say

about sorrow and regret and how horrible the ocean seemed because it would stay between us forever, she interrupted, to say, in Peter Santore's voice, "Bye, Hilary. Bye-bye." And then, in hers, she answered: "Bye."

Which left me with a dead phone that lay across a chest that wasn't, no matter what I might work at convincing myself to wish for, dead. I suppose that's another part of the curse. I hung the phone up and set it on the carpet next to the bed. I waited for the knocking to tell me that Fox had arrived. It didn't. I stared at nothing in the dark, prepared to wait for him and think about Hilary. What I did, soft American boy, was fall asleep and sleep until the squeak of tea carts in the corridor told me that Fox hadn't come in the night, and the night was over, and I was alive and must fly.

It was easy to pack, since half of my luggage was in Salisbury. In the shower I winced, and as I shaved I was ginger in the way I stretched or turned. I put clean clothes on a stiff, sore body and, holding myself as if I were a jar that someone must not drop because it was fragile, I brought myself downstairs, passing the great, stretched picture of where I had been and where it had occurred to me to stay, and I went along and paid.

In Heathrow, I walked through family after family, among all those alarmed children and exhausted parents, in the high, bright plastic cathedral of saying farewell, until I found a seat aboard an Air Canada flight to New York that left in two hours. I bought aspirin and coffee and croissants, and dipped my sportcoat sleeve in spilled fruit juice as I ate, managing the feeding motions awkwardly, wincing as I tilted back to drain the last of the coffee with too much sugar and milk.

He found me at the duty-free shop. I had just finished purchasing Laphroaig for Bert and Vent Vert for my mother, when I smelled sharp mints and bad cheese, and felt a stiff jab in the ribs that nearly moved me back through the duty-free counter. I winced and hugged myself, and then I turned.

What else could I say except, "Well, hello dere, Kingfish."

"Are you unwell, old man?" He motioned with the hand that had just dropped down from wiping his eye, pointing at the arm with which I held myself.

I shook my head. "I'm great," I said.

"Thought I owed it to us all to see you off." He was wearing a light gray herringbone tweed jacket I was jealous of, and glossy black loafers, gray flannels with creases you could have used for plowing snow. His dark blue paisley tie and blue oxford shirt were unwrinkled. I wondered if he'd changed after driving to Heathrow from Winchester— or had it been from her cottage? "They told me at the hotel you'd left. I had hoped we might chat."

"Jesus, Fox," I said.

"Mister Fox, I think," he said. "Or, better, Sergeant-Major Fox. But Jesus Fox won't do, and neither will Fox, and neither, telling you the truth, will Jesus."

"What in hell could we want to say to each other? You told me all about my father's contribution to the passing parade. And you made it clear what you'd gone through.

And you managed to convince me that Hilary's a bit busy these days."

"You found us in our privacy."

"You loved it."

I was gasping. I prevented myself from bending double and going to the floor by reciting famous landmark Constitutional decisions.

"You shouldn't have come, of course," he said. "Or been born. Did your mother mate after our quisling had turned his true coat, or are you the product of a legal and legitimate coupling between the man without a country and some cunt without a man?"

"Brown versus Topeka Board of Education," I said.

He stared at me with his wet eyes. He stepped toward me, and toward me again, then closer. I winced in advance, as if I knew he was going to hit me across the throat, or jab me in the solar plexus, or knee me in the balls. I cringed. But he stepped in even closer, so that he was all but leaning against me. The smell of his awful teeth came through the screen of candies he'd crunched, hard candies, I supposed, because they seemed to have drawn blood which glazed his healthy middle teeth. The smell of rotten gums and blood and brown loose teeth, and of all his secrets in their secret places, came up to me. And then his hands came out and gripped my face. I couldn't move. His face came in on mine, and then his mouth lay against my lips and he pressed them, pressed in past them with his teeth and tongue until I tore away, fell back, lay partly on my aching side against the glass counter of the duty-free.

I couldn't draw a breath without feeling ice throughout

my chest. I felt foul, and ashamed, and I knew that I'd wish to have hit him. And I knew how frightened I was to try.

The woman in pink behind the counter said, "We *never* allow that."

Fox loomed again, but didn't touch me. His dark cave of ruined teeth said, close to my own, "Fucking her one door away from you was almost as good as fucking you would have been. And fucking you would have brought me dearly near to fucking your dear old dad."

He stepped back, and the sound of his seething breath and the stink of his dying teeth receded. I clamped my arms at my sides and folded my hands against my chest. The woman behind us said, coldly, "Please take your receipt when you leave, sir."

"Still," Fox said, "we can't have everything, can we? We are, after all, civilized." He shot his cuffs. "Hilary sends you her best," he said.

I said, "She sent me what she could. I don't think she has a lot left for anyone."

I did remember my receipt. I even tried to nod to the woman who gave it to me. I walked away from him stiffly, and I headed for a flight of stairs I didn't want. I took them anyway. I was on a balcony high above the departures terminal, and from it, when I mustered the courage to turn and look down, I could see Fox's squared shoulders and straight back as he walked through a long queue of slowly shuffling travelers, and, after too long for my liking, out. My arm and shoulder ached, but they would have to wait their turn for any more attention. I wanted a drink, of bleach, preferably, but there wasn't time. It seemed, from the way a very short, dour woman in a yellow sari looked at me, that I was weeping. Like Fox, I reached to wipe my eyes. I could not imagine how to tell someone in a yellow sari, or in a roundheeled intellectual's outfit, or a sharp tweed sportcoat, what I was weeping for. I could not imagine knowing.

I sniffed and wiped my eyes again. I went downstairs and carried my ticket and my luggage check, my claim slip for my duty-free goods, my sore curving body, my burning mouth, and the book I'd brought for the trip to the line I was to stand in. I wondered if my father had made his long flight with tears in his eyes. I wondered why he had tried to come back from so far away. I shuffled forward with the line, and they checked that we carried valid passports, and then they took our tickets, and then we went on board. I sat at an emergency exit, near a stewardess' station, and my double row was occupied only by me. I sat and buckled in and waited for the long patter, then the takeoff, then the flight.

They were cheering us aboard in French, and then in German. I held the book, balanced it, turned it—a new object, a heavy gift of puzzling function and design. It mattered because she had showed me Stonehenge and had lain, a sacrifice, on the stone. "Remember this," she'd said. The book mattered because she had written in it. I opened its pages and read, again, alone in the burr of foreign languages, its title: *Tess of the D'Urbervilles: A Pure Woman.* I had never noticed the subtitle. She had never spoken it. I might read it all. I could finish it before we landed home. I could sit, and not sleep. I could read every page, each sentence, every word, from "On an evening in the latter part of May," through—I pulled at pages, turned great chunks of book—until "two speechless gazers bent themselves down to the earth, as if in prayer, and remained thus a long time, absolutely motionless: the flag continued to wave silently. As soon as they had strength they arose, joined hands again, and went on."

The stewardess told us in English how welcome we were. I could read the dust wrapper, too, and the copyright page, all of it, from *"First published, 1891"* to *"THE END."* I would have to skip her looped and tangled inscription, though. I had no hands to join but my own. I clasped them over the closed book, sealing away the signature of Hilary's warning or wish. Soon enough we flew.

Frederick Busch

Born in Brooklyn, New York, and educated at Muhlenberg College and Columbia University, Frederick Busch has since 1971 published 24 books. His novels include *The Mutual Friend*, about Charles Dickens, as well as *Rounds*, *Harry and Catherine*, *Closing Arguments*, *Girls*, and *The Night Inspector* (1999). Volumes of short fiction include *Too Late American Boyhood Blues*, *Absent Friends*, *The Children in the Woods*: *New and Selected Stories*, and *Don't Tell Anyone* (October, 2000). He has received the Woodrow Wilson, Ingram Merrill, National Endowment for the Arts, and Guggenheim Fellowships, and has been awarded the PEN/Malamud Award for Achievement in the Short Story. He has also been honored for his body of work by the American Academy of Arts and Letters and has been awarded the National Jewish Book Award for his novel *Invisible Mending*. His stories are widely anthologized in annual editions of *The O. Henry Awards*, *The Best American Short Stories* and *The Pushcart Prize*, and regularly appear in magazines and journals including *The New Yorker*, *Harper's*, *Zoetrope*, *Georgia Review* and *The Threepenny Review*, among others.

Busch has served as acting director of the Writers' Workshop at the University of Iowa, and has lectured and read from his work extensively. He is Fairchild Professor of Literature at Colgate University, where he teaches literature and fiction writing and conducts the Living Writers course. He and his wife Judy, the parents of two grown sons, live in Upstate New York.